THE MOTHER'S SECRET

VICTORIAN ROMANCE

SADIE HOPE

A MOTHER'S SECRET

This is a romance set in the dismal streets of Victorian London. I hope you will enjoy my stories as I share them with you. I have only just started sharing my writing and am still learning. I do appreciate you my readers, for all the wonderful feedback I have received.

Some of you love the fact that I have serialised these books about Valeria, Allen, and Nora, others have not been so happy

I decided to do it this way as you, my readers, were asking for stories and this way it was easier to get them out quickly.

Each book can be read alone, and has its own story, but if you wish to read them from the start they are:

The Orphan's Courage

The Orphan's Hope

The Mother's Secret

The Maid's Blessing

Sadie Hope

https://www.facebook.com/AuthorSadieHope/

Join my newsletter for new release announcements and special offers
http://eepurl.com/dOVZDb

CHAPTER ONE

*V*aleria tried the door to her room again. It remained locked, shutting her in her own little prison. Since Allen had broken into Miss Umbridge's desk in the library this had been the state of things. It stung. She had trusted the boy and he had betrayed her. Worse than that, Miss Umbridge believed that she had colluded with him. This had been her chance at a good life and it was taken away by the boy she thought was her friend. The boy she thought she loved.

Now, Valeria was confined to her room during her free hours. Before, she had used these for self-improvement, reading, or walking into the countryside to the North or the great city of London to the South.

She could tell that Cook didn't agree with her punishment. She didn't like acting as her turnkey. Imprisoning her in this room whenever she couldn't keep close watch in person. No matter how firm Cook tried to be, the worry lines on her face gave her away. She couldn't hide how much she hated to do this, but the act of distrust still hurt Valeria, even though Cook didn't share the feelings of distrust behind it. Miss Umbridge had decreed that if Cook, or one of the other household staff were not about to act as chaperone to Valeria then Valeria was to be kept in her room under physical incarceration until someone could take over and keep watch.

In practice this whole task had fallen on Cook's shoulders.

The door now checked for the fifth or sixth time that hour, Valeria returned to her bed. This was how she passed the time; pacing, trying the door, napping, pacing some more and reading.

She was still allowed to access the library, which was a blessed relief. Like the locked doors, it stung that

Deloris no longer kept anything of value in there along with the late Mr. Umbridge's vast collection of books.

This was all the reading she did now, Deloris no longer treated her as a companion... as a daughter as she had begun to do. Once she had even mentioned the possibility of adoption. It had been an offhand comment as was often the case. Miss Umbridge had asked her opinion of being adopted by her.

It had taken Valeria's breath away and she had fought hard to keep the grin off her face. She had answered that she would love the idea and would find it a great honour. Delores had said that she would think about it.

Only now things had changed for the worst. The easy relationship and friendship they shared was gone. That was what hurt the most. Once she had been the closest thing to a mother that Valeria could remember and now, she was little more than a stranger... her employer... and one who distrusted her deeply. Of course, she understood how hurt Delores must be and she hated Allen for that.

Miss Umbrigde no longer asked Valeria to read to

her, nor was Valeria called on to make conversation on whatever cultural artifact Miss Umbridge had decided she wanted to share her own opinion on.

However, as a prisoner in this home she would take what she could get and her studies, entertainments, monographs, dictionaries, translations, collations, catalogs, romances, essays and epics helped to pass the time when she was not scrubbing windows or sweeping floors. It was still a much better life than the orphanage where she had grown up... if only she hadn't trusted Allen.

Idly flipping through the pages of a few books, Valeria eventually settled on the slim, paperbound copy of Marx's *Manifesto*. Much of her reading of late had been revolutionary in nature. There was something thrilling about this possibility for change that made her feel almost as if she might one day be free of that wretched door and its ever-locked handle.

A noise pulled her out of the book, it was coming from the front of the house. Listening, Valeria heard the big front entrance open and close behind someone. Soon after that came the creak of the stairs as Cook ascended them. From the direction of her footsteps on the landing she wasn't coming straight to let Valeria out. Instead, the footsteps moved in the opposite direction, to Miss Umbridge's room.

Valeria wondered how the old woman was. She understood the feeling of betrayal that her employer must feel. She knew how the situation looked. Instead of hating the old lady, Valeria's entire bitterness about the injustice of her plight had fallen on Allen, who had sold her out for a handful of corporate paper.

Anger flared again as she wondered why he had done it. Although, if she were honest, she knew little of him. A few stolen meetings late at night at the orphanage. A shared lack of trust and empathy about their upbringing had led her to believe that he was a friend. More than that... those nights she had waited for him, the thrill of seeing the black-haired boy with the eyes so blue she could drown in them. It had all been in her mind. A silly childish romance that had let her believe he was her friend... even after he tried to lift her purse and after he had told her he was a pickpocket. Why would she expect anything but treachery? That was logical, what wasn't was the sense of loss and betrayal his actions had caused.

Valeria returned to her book, reading silently to herself in her head. Enjoying the grandiose and high-handed prose of the philosopher-historian who she had once seen hunched over some ancient volume in the reading room of the British Museum.

His words had stuck with her.

"The history of all hitherto existing society is the history of class struggles."

That certainly felt like the struggles she was experiencing. Locked up by a woman whose only power over her came from her birth. It felt remarkable to have such an authoritative voice state, without equivocation, that her daily life was in some way a reflection of the great driving force of history.

Now, the words on the page spoke to her and spoke of her lack of control.

Freeman and slave, patrician and plebeian, lord and serf, guild-master and journeyman, in a word, oppressor and oppressed, stood in constant opposition to one another, carried on an uninterrupted, now hidden, now open fight, a fight that each time ended, either in a revolutionary reconstitution of society at large, or in the common ruin of the contending classes. In the earlier epochs of history, we find almost everywhere a complicated arrangement of society into various orders, a manifold gradation of social rank...

She had learned to read silently, in her own head, the skill had come to her after Allen had ruined her friendship with Miss Umbridge. With no one to read to, she had learned to sink inside herself and read there. Making no noise with her words she didn't worry who would hear and what they would think.

The author seemed to be calling for a violent overthrow of the ruling classes. That seemed a bit strong to Valeria. She wasn't sure she wanted to see Miss Umbridge ruined or cast down. In fact, most of her anger was towards Miss June and Allen, who could hardly be said to be members of the "bourgeois" classes.

Shifting how she sat on the bed, she tried to concentrate on the writing but that word *plebeian* nagged at her. She couldn't quite remember its meaning, knowing only that it was Latin. She longed to consult the dictionaries in the library, but instead was stuck here. Though it was large and beautiful, the empty room felt ever more and more like a closet

— or even a prison cell — as the love she had felt in the house seemed to have melted away.

It struck her as extraordinary that a little affection could so change the feel and emotional texture of an inanimate place. As if there were a further architecture of love that was laid over a building by those who lived, and worked, and were held within its walls.

Valeria pushed the book aside, unable to concentrate on the class struggle. She got up and tried the door handle again futilely, knowing it was locked, but trying all the same. She could see herself doing it again and again, sometimes in the past, sometimes in the future. All these small actions that seemed to be building towards the one time it would be unlocked.

And if it were unlocked — when that day finally came — would she just walk away? She feared terribly that it was not just that lock that held her in place. She could have escaped Miss June's orphanage and lived on the street. A rough life, but it couldn't have been worse than Miss June's tortures. She hadn't left then, none of them had. Perhaps there was more to bondage than just chains and guards.

She let go the handle, and as she did so a sound came to her, carried a little by the pipes which ran through the ceiling above her room. Footsteps. The familiar sound of Cookie on the stairs.

Finally, she thought. Cookie coming to my rescue from the lock that Cookie herself had locked. It seemed odd to think of Cook as a rescuer, for to do so made her both dragon and knight. But then again, Valeria was finding all her emotions and impressions more and more mixed up of late.

With her imprisonment, the worlds of her reading and of her dreams had become more real and sometimes seemed to live around her. When she put the books away or woke from her slumbers they still hovered in the corners of her eyes. She felt love for Allen, and hate. Love for Miss Umbridge, and hate. And for Cookie she felt the ire of the prisoner and the gratitude of the liberated.

Sure enough she soon heard that familiar step in the corridor outside her room, perhaps a little cheerier than usual, but certainly the gait of Cookie none the less.

The key scraped in the lock and Cookie appeared, her smile beaming out of her face.

"Well now, Miss Valeria. I have a little treat for you. It took a fair bit of persuading from the mistress mind, but she's amenable to reason and wants to see the good in folks. So, I finally talked her round."

Valeria's heart leaped. "Oh, Cookie. What have you managed to persuade her of?"

"Well, now. She's not convinced you're innocent yet. And it's a small concession. But I was talking about these dangerous books you've been reading." She gestured at the pile which currently contained the titles *On Liberty*, *Common Sense*, *A Vindication on the Rights of Women*, and the first volume of Louis Blanc's account of the French Revolution.

"Dangerous books?" Valeria asked.

Revolutionary to be sure, thought Valeria, but dangerous? What could one girl do to change the world the way these books described?

To Valeria these books were like the stories told in Mallory or *Beowulf*, they were fantastical lands where everything was turned topsy turvy by evil wizards and supernatural heroes. The utopia of Marx was to her no more real than Homer's land of the dead. But she loved to dream and those dreams did sometimes seem more real than the walls around her.

"Aye, deadly in some cases. I know how it went with the French, Dearie. I picked up enough history from my school ma'ams and Miss Umbridge to know that revolution and liberalism are not ideas for a young lady of your station to be reading."

"What did Miss Umbridge say about these books when you told her what I'd been reading?"

"She said nothing. Well, not nothing exactly. She laughed at the thought of you bearing a tricolour and storming the barricades. Then she said to me, 'Well, Cookie. We'll have to do some remedial work. Have her bring one up to read to me again.' Or something along those lines, you know the way she talks. And of late she's become ever so confusing and confused. Repeats things all the time. But she can bear to see you again, which is the first step to a reconciliation between you two."

"Is this true?"

Cook gave one of her beautiful smiles as she bustled into the room. "It is, so, I came here to tell you the good news. She still wants you locked up or kept an eye on, and there's still no going to town for you. At least not any more than you already have in the last month or so. But it seems she can stomach the sight of you again so I guess she is feeling less likely to throw you to the law or the wolves."

Valeria listened to all this with a deep sense of gratefulness in her heart. Though she felt the sting of those last few words, she was finally given a chance to see Miss Umbridge in person and perhaps make some movement towards rekindling her trust and affection.

After all, it was much easier to hate a person in absentia than when confronted by the humanity of their face.

Was that her own reason for anger? No, she was justified in her fury at Allen. Still, with this gesture of forgiveness, she similarly let go of some of her rage towards the boy. He who had truly betrayed her in almost exactly the way Miss Umbridge mistakenly believed she had been betrayed.

"In the meantime, come give Cookie a hand with beating the carpets now. It'll be good for you to get out the house and see some green. To breathe some fresh air." Cook gave a chuckle. "Even if it is clouded with the dust off the carpets."

Valeria laughed along with Cook and rose, and straightening out her maid's uniform, she obediently following Cookie downstairs.

CHAPTER TWO

Valeria had finished the task of beating the carpets and had come back into the house to clean the inside of the windows in the front rooms. An hour and a half had passed, according to the clock on the mantle which had been known to run slow, when Mr Wright arrived.

Valeria's heart sank at the sound of his voice, speaking with Miss Umbridge's butler in the hallway in that charming way he had. She loathed all his good qualities for how completely they served to mask his bad qualities from those around him.

Plunging her sponge back into the ice-cold bucket of water, she tried to ignore the sound of his voice. Proper and cultured and yet she could hear an undercurrent of vice. In her heart she willed him to go straight to the library. It was what he usually did if Valeria was not available to force his presence upon.

Hard as she willed it, she could not avoid hearing Mr Wright pronounce her name to the footman and her heart sank. He would be asking her location and would then appear in the room as if by coincidence, telling her that he was simply waiting for their joint mistress.

Sure enough, a few moments later Mr Wright entered the room and began his ridiculous charade.

Valeria turned and curtseyed, exchanged the minimal pleasantries required for good form and then returned to cleaning the windows.

Rubbing hard, she looked out through the glass, but the view was obscured by the smears from vinegar and newspaper. The hair on her neck stood on end as she felt, rather than heard, him approach. It was a movement of air and a sense of human warmth at her back. He stood so close behind her that she could feel his breath on her neck. The man was far closer than was appropriate.

"Are you cold, Miss Collins? You are positively shaking."

She could hear his smile in his voice.

"No, Sir. It is just my hands; this vinegar is rather chilly." She leaned down for the bucket and felt him take a half step back, to admire the way her hips would move as she bent at the waist. Instead of bending she crouched down.

When she looked up, she could see that stare of his, investigating her body like it was one of his legal documents. Narrow eyes peered through the dark framed glasses, not looking for flaws but admiring her as his tongue flicked over his wide lips. No doubt he felt that such a stare was a compliment, appreciative of her beauty. But she knew the real thoughts behind it.

One of Miss June's favourite Bible quotations was from Matthew five. *Ye have heard that it was said by them of old time, 'Thou shalt not commit adultery'; but I say unto you, that whosoever looketh on a woman to lust after her hath committed adultery with her already in his heart.*

She couldn't shake the fear that Miss June had

instilled in her that the sin applied as much to the woman as the man. That the sin, if not already committed, was soon to be so. Mr Wright had a way of making her feel uncomfortable, afraid, and ashamed, whenever he was in a room with her.

Giving the last few smears a polish with rolled up paper she threw it into the pail and moved quickly to the next window. Mr Wright, to Valeria's relief remained standing where he was.

Increasingly, his behaviour had taken on this style.

He would find her when she was alone and try to talk with her, always radiating confidence and charm which he thought she couldn't resist. Other times he would simply watch her. Watching her every movement with a look that seemed twisted beyond desire into a kind of physical pain. But he never did anything that would give her chance to complain. There was nothing tangible, just a feeling. He never touched her, beyond the assistance a gentleman might offer a lady. He never suggested anything that might cross the rules of society. But he would stare without shame at any part of her he chose and stand so close she could feel his breath on her neck.

"You missed a bit," he said, gesturing at the window without taking his eyes off her chest. "You really must be more thorough. Give it a good scrub. Put your back into it. After all, the only way to win over the lady of the house is hard work done well."

He was right about the window, in her efforts to escape his proximity she had left a full pane of glass murky with dust. Reluctantly, she took a step back towards him.

He did not move although he stood so close to the window she had to make herself most thin in order not to touch either the wet glass or the unpleasant warmness of Mr Wright.

"Allow me," he said. Unfolding her small step ladder and placing it conveniently on the ground before the window.

Holding her breath, she stepped onto it and was aware of his eye line watching the hem of her dress for the moment her shoes appeared to clear the step. There was a fearsome intensity in his gaze.

"A woman at work is a beautiful sight, Miss Collins. Many women of my acquaintance do nothing all day but gossip and sew. Even the most comely of them lack the simple ability to complete such a simple and menial task.

"Thank you, Sir," she said feeling how tight her lips were about the words. She felt disgusted by the way he licked his lips and how his eyes shone with lust. It brought back a memory of Allen's hand on her waist as they had walked up to the house. There had been joy at that contact.

Rubbing the bunched up newspaper over the pane again and again she dreaded the moment when she knew Mr Wright would help her down from the ladder. When he would place his hand on the same place that Allen had. How different the two touches were.

"You know, I for one do not believe you brought that boy into this house to rob it," he said as she scrubbed the window. "You were merely a victim of your own good nature. Some men — and indeed boys — will do all they can to charm and flatter, and many women of your tender age are prone to listen to their sweet nothings. Though I could tell at once that he was of the lower... dare I say, the criminal classes, I felt I could say nothing to a boy you had offered Miss Umbridge's hospitality to."

This was not the first time he had tried this tactic. She understood that something about Allen had upset him and until he was sure she blamed Allen totally for her woes Mr Wright would not be happy. So, she did her best to not let him know that he was absolutely correct. That she had believed Allen's lies and allowed him to scout the house out and break not only the integrity of the house but the status it had held for her as a home.

She hated Mr Wright even more for this. That he was so right about her situation felt like the final insult. That one as abhorrent as him, could be right about Allen being corrupt, was like the final nail in her coffin of despair.

When she stepped down from the ladder and he touched her again she understood just how little difference his being right about Allen made to the grand scheme of unpleasantness. Trying to make it look like an accident she slipped towards him a little way and spilled the full cup of vinegar down his front.

It was a foolish act and could leave her in even more trouble and yet it made her feel just a little more in control.

CHAPTER THREE

Allen was back at it. Picking pockets. It was no longer for practice the way it used to be. Then he would just grab the odd coin purse or wallet just to keep the fingers loose and the wits honed. Just enough to get by. Now this was his full-time occupation, all day every day, unless Taylor gave him something worse to do.

This was his job now — his dangerous, badly paying job. Though he tried to take from those who could afford it, he couldn't always do so. To survive himself he couldn't be too picky. So, more often than not he was taking the hard-earned wages of those not all that much better off than himself. It filled him with shame, but that wasn't why he hated it so much. No, the reason he hated picking pockets so much was that he had to do it for Taylor.

The man had been saviour at first. Helping him when he needed it most. When he had been chased from the orphanage and had nowhere to go. Taylor acted like a knight in shining armour. Plucking him from the depths of despair. Over the following weeks he acted like a father, a mentor, and finally when the chips were down a tyrant. Once Allen was in his debt things had changed and Allen had found that to defy Taylor could be deadly for his friends. Though he wanted to run, he believed that to leave Taylor would be very dangerous and it would mean he would be running for the rest of his life.

Allen was so tired of running. Running from the police, running from Taylor's punishments, running from marks that spotted him, running as fast as he could just to be allowed to keep on running.

Allen had to contribute to the gang and the pickings were far thinner cutting purses than they were for breaking and entering. It meant his takings were often looked at with disdain. Every evening as he traipsed home with the lining of his coat full of coins he was filled with fear. Not that the purses and wallets he had discarded in dark places about the town would be discovered; no, his fear was far worse. Every evening he wondered if today would be the day —the one when Taylor decided he was more use blinded and begging than lifting purses. Allen had seen one of the gang that didn't bring in much coin, a young boy who was supposed to have left of his own accord... only Allen had seen him on the street... with his eyes cut out and a bowl in his hands for the alms.

Sometimes he wondered if that would be the best way. Then at least the struggle would stop. Allen thought this to himself, saying the words, *at least the struggle will stop*, in his head in time to his footsteps down the cobbles of the street.

With his eyes put out, he could just slide into the darkness and take the coins that were passed to him from out there in the pitch black. There was no point in running when you were blind, no need to as a beggar. He could finally stop, stand still, and let fate take over.

But somehow the thought still appalled and terrified him. When he thought of that poor boy, the one he couldn't help. So he would keep running, and keep doing as little harm as he could until his legs gave out, either metaphorically or literally. Then the world could make the final decision for him.

Today was going particularly poorly from the point of view of his take. The weather was cold and Allen was clumsier as a result. He'd passed up a couple of easy targets because they looked hungry and desperate. The few coins they had they needed. Then he had missed others because his hands were numb or — much worse — shaking, and now he had to go back to Taylor with just a few coins. Fear placed a chill, far colder even than the weather, in his stomach.

Taylor had beaten him a few times for coming home without enough cash in his coat, sometimes Taylor had beaten him just for coming home. The man hated Allen and had done ever since that night. The one when — Allen hated to think of it — he had robbed Valeria.

Jingling the coins in his pocket he wondered what to do. Maybe he could stay out late, but then he would miss dinner and Taylor had already greatly reduced his rations. So, he headed back, hoping to find one good mark before he was done.

The walk took him past the nice part of town. The part where Valeria lived and his guilt was back. He knew that it was not his friend he had stolen from. Not really. He had taken from the kind old lady who kept Valeria like some sort of caged songbird.

There was very little guilt for the small dent he had made in the vast holdings of one of England's wealthier types. No, the guilt was for Valeria. Though he knew the damage he had done to her might not be financial, he also knew it would hurt all the more because it came from him.

She had given him trust, brought him into her home, given him food, and he had returned as a thief in the night to steal from the household of those who had given to him freely.

Despite the damage he had done it was not enough. Taylor's words were burned into his mind.

"You wretched little ingrate," Taylor had said eyeing up the half dozen bonds Allen had liberated from Miss Umbridge's library. It was still nearly one-hundred-and-twenty-pounds worth of bonds. A little more than that if Taylor waited and collected the interest vouchers before redeeming them. That was enough for a man to live nicely for three or four years without having to labour.

But there was fear behind Taylor's anger when he looked at the pile and swept them up.

For the first time, Allen began to realise that there might be someone above Taylor. That even bosses have their bosses all the way up to the Queen, and her boss was simply God. This great unseen person hung down from those celestial heights and Allen was the bottommost link. No one looked up to him, and he looked up to everyone. He was the one who would get stomped if there was stomping to be done.

Seeing that fear made things worse. If it were Taylor who was pocketing the money, Allen could be sure of getting a fair cut. But it was clear that Taylor owed a cut to his boss and the one-hundred-and-twenty pounds on the table between them wouldn't keep the bigger fish from eating him alive. At least not for long.

"You wretched little ingrate," Taylor had said.

Allen could have cried. Didn't Taylor know what he had done, how much he had given up, broken, who he had done this to? Taylor could only see the summed-up pounds, shillings, and pennies. That was all Taylor had ever been able to see. Even as Allen had looked up to him as a father, Taylor had been looking back at him and seeing an investment, a pile of coins that would either yield a return of interest that could be measured in pounds, shillings and pennies or would have to be broken up and sold on to recover whatever could be recovered in the dimensions of pounds, shillings and pennies.

There was no human warmth to be had in a mind made all of copper, silver and gold.

After the debacle at Miss Umbridge's Allen was put on starvation rations and given poor little side streets to work. Everyone else on Taylor's crew were put on overtime trying to make up the shortfall.

Taylor had clearly promised the Umbridge fortune to someone dangerous and they were not taking excuses as payment in kind.

Naturally, Taylor ensured all the blame for the other gang member's hardships was squarely placed at the door of poor Allen. They all viewed it as his fault and never suspected that Taylor might be as afraid of failing the man above him as they were of failing him.

So here he was, pockets almost empty and walking back through the great thoroughfares of the greatest city on earth where money moved in vast streams around him. If only he could figure out how to dip his cup in and draw out enough to find some measure of freedom. He looked up at the beautiful new buildings that had gone up where Baker Street met Grosvenor Square and stopped. An old man was just getting out of a carriage, his frail legs carrying him to the pavement only under considerable duress. The poor fellow looked about ready to pitch sideways into the gutter at the slightest gust of wind, and his clumsy old hands were struggling to get his purse out of his coat to pay the cabbie.

He may have looked poorly, but he was certainly not poor, the man's coat was beautifully tailored and his top hat shone brightly with the polish of silk and quicksilver. As Allen got closer, he could see the soft leather of the man's gloves and the fine white fur of his coat lining. All signs suggested that this man's pocket, once picked, might well offer a solution to the very worst aspects of Allen's predicament.

Breath held, Allen watched for a moment, walking closer and closer to the old man, until he was almost under the shadow of the coachman's horse. The old man paid up his fare and slid the purse into the inside pocket of his coat.

It looked like an easy lift to Allen who moved to bump the old man a little as he walked past, but as if by the hand of providence, just as he was about to bump the man the purse fell out of his coat without any influence from Allen.

The old coot had put it in his pocket wrong. Without having to touch the nest, Allen had been delivered the eggs. Even though the purse hit the floor with what sounded like an almighty thud making the coins chink loudly, the man didn't turn to pick it up.

A loud purse is a full one, Allen thought.

The cabbie pulling away made such a rattling on the cobblestones that the old man had completely failed to hear his loss.

Allen paused anxiously, the old man kept walking. Then he stepped forward and bent down, grabbing the purse, and quickly slipping it into his pocket. It was so easy. It had been a full day of eking out every possible penny, using every trick at his disposal and sneaking from crime to crime with every terror of being caught. Then he had been delivered a paycheque at the last hour of his day that made all his labours worthwhile — he could tell just how worthwhile by the way the purse pulled his coat askew on his shoulders. That kind of weight in a purse that small spoke of at least two or three guineas, quite possibly more.

Allen started to walk away from his crime, casually, hands in his trouser pockets. He even began to hum an old song he remembered hearing as a child that spun Napoleon Buonaparte into a bogeyman that kept children on the straight and narrow.

"Baby, baby, he's a giant, tall and black as church's steeples

And he dines and sups, rely on't, every night on naughty people.

Baby, baby, he will hear you, as he passes by the house,

And he, limb from limb, will tear you...

Just as pussy tears. A. Mouse."

As he reached the end of the verse, he felt a hand close on his shoulder and a voice speak from behind him.

"Boy!" the voice cried. "Put that purse back."

The voice was too young and vigorous to be the old man, the grip on his shoulder too strong. He turned to see a young man who had come up the street behind him.

I must be tired, Allen thought. Not to have checked the street before I grabbed the purse.

Allen jerked to one side shaking free of the man's grip and taking a step back. He paused for a moment wondering what best to do. Could he talk his way out of this? Tell the man he'd grabbed the purse for the old man. To return it, not to steal it.

A quick glance at how much ground he'd covered in the wrong direction told him this story would be a hard sell.

The younger man, as if trying not to startle an animal paused and took a slow half step forward to bring himself back in range to make another grab at Allen.

Allen had no such tentativeness in his actions. Talking

was off the table and tired as he was of running, it was clear that now was the time to get back to it.

Allen legged it.

He was tired from running, tired of running, but not too tired to run. He could tell when running became the only choice, when everything cleverer might fail, there was always the option to retreat. He would make no tentative half-steps like his pursuer.

As fast as he could, he shot across Baker Street and down a side road, looking about frantically for a place to hide before his pursuer made the corner and forced him to run all the way to the next turning or alleyway to try and lose him.

It took him a moment to scan the rows of almost identical terraced houses with their iron fences that enclosed just a few feet of lawn.

He spotted a nicely terraced house with an open window on the ground floor, and taking a gamble, climbed onto the low fence. It took great dexterity of foot to avoid being skewered on the spikes but he managed to get his feet carefully standing between the spikes, and he leaped for the window sill.

THE MOTHER'S SECRET

It would have been an easy landing but he had not been as careful as he thought and the spikes on the fence caught his trousers causing him to stumble forwards. So, instead of ducking under the sash and rolling gracefully onto the floor of the room, he slammed his head into the sash hard enough to crack the pane of glass above it, his legs went on without him and he was spun onto his back crashing onto the window ledge.

With his head in a blinding agony and seeing spots he rolled himself through the window and onto the small chess table below the sill. This table promptly collapsed and planted him firmly on the floor with a bishop violently prodding his ribs and a rook jabbing at his fundament.

It took a moment for his head to clear, and when he looked up, he was staring at a truly terrifying man, whose severe expression seemed to burn into Allen's bruised skull.

With a voice that seemed to express the deepest contempt for Allen's lowly state the man said, "My apologies, young Sir. We were not expecting visitors this afternoon. However, should you wish to pay a call in the future, this house, like many others, is possessed of a doorbell and a front door."

"I was... I had to..." Allen tried to explain, or at the very least provide an excuse for why he had come through a stranger's window.

"Quite," said the angry man. "You should perhaps, come with me, I expect the Master will want to meet you before we have you hung for burgling." He looked past Allen to the scattered pieces of the table. "And for causing such a mess."

Allen's gut went cold and he looked back at the window. He could hear feet on the street, the man was still searching for him. Should he run and risk being caught again? No, he had a better chance of talking *the Master* out of hanging him than the man outside so he meekly got to his feet and followed.

CHAPTER FOUR

Nora became Mrs Richmond in the Spring. The wedding was a small one, in Richmond's home town, the place of his childhood and the realm ruled over by the patriarchs and matriarchs of the Richmond family.

How far she had come, from an orphanage to being married to a gentleman. It was a dream come true. The only thing that could have made it better would be to see her friend again. Valeria had been like a sister to her and had visited the orphanage occasionally after she was given the position of companion to a wealthy old lady. Only, once William Richmond had taken Nora from the orphanage, she had lost touch with her friend. There seemed no way to find out how she was doing.

For the service Nora was outfitted in carefully tailored pink muslin patterned over with white lace. To complete the outfit, she had a long shawl of white — like the Queen had worn at her wedding back in eighteen-forty.

Atop her head she wore a bonnet on which were wreathed various hothouse flowers cut from the laboratories of Mr Richmond — her William as she had taken to calling him now. She wanted holly in the wreath but even in the town of Hamley-on-Thames on the far outskirts of London there was little by way of wildflowers or holly berries to be found, especially at this time of year.

It didn't matter, she felt like a princess and one who was about to marry her prince. Even in her wildest dreams with Valeria she would never have imagined being so happy. William treated her well as an employee but gradually they had fallen in love. It happened over his experiments and she found herself as interested in it all as he was. When he had rescued her from the jealous Miss June, the owner of the orphanage, it had been a dream come true. Then as time went on, they became friends and then fell in love. Nora had to keep pinching herself to be convinced this was not a dream.

The service was held at the Richmond's family church, St Mary's. A Catholic church, newly built and barely fifty-years-old. It stood in glorious red-bricked defiance of the protestant parish church, the spire of which was visible from the consecrated ground of St Mary's with its scattering of ornate tombstones. Catholicism in this town was an eccentricity only of the wealthy and so the church had prospered.

A fat looking priest in black read from Genesis on the creation of Eve. "Therefore, shall a man leave his father and his mother, and shall cleave unto his wife: and they shall be one flesh."

In the tale of the fall of woman, in the Garden of Eden, Nora found little to delight. Instead, she remembered the verse of St Paul on charitable love.

Love suffereth long, and is kind; love envieth not, love vaunteth not itself, is not puffed up, it doth not behave itself unseemly, seeketh not her own, is not easily provoked, thinketh no evil, rejoiceth not in iniquity, but rejoiceth in the truth, beareth all things, believeth all things, hopeth all things, endureth all things,"

It had been one of the few lessons Miss June had taught them that had stuck. It had felt real, and kind and not rooted in some cruel desire to make all the girls not only suffer more, but believe that they must suffer to be good. Well, she was going to suffer no longer. She was determined of that. She had found a love that was kind, and she loved the rhythm of the passage.

Love never faileth: but whether there be prophecies, they shall fail, whether there be tongues, they shall cease, whether there be knowledge, it shall vanish away.

When she and Valeria had learned it, it had taken on a talismanic effect, the idea that thought.

We know only in part, and we prophesy only in part, when that which is perfect is come, then that which is in part shall be done away. When I was a child, I spake as a child, I understood as a child, I thought as a child: but when I became a man, I put away childish things.

Perhaps this mythical version of love was a childish

thing, but it would not be put away for anything. Not for all the fruit in Eden.

If I have a faith that can move mountains, but do not have love, I am nothing If I give all I possess to the poor and give over my body to hardship that I may boast, but do not have love, I gain nothing.

Love is patient, love is kind. It does not envy, it does not boast, it is not proud.

She recited the passage silently under her veil even as the priest read his words in Latin.

The church behind the couple was almost empty.

None of the Richmond had deigned to attend the wedding. Even those that wanted to had been warned off by the elders of the family.

Nora had read the letter William's mother wrote describing William marrying Nora as being, *a dreadful debasement of the family name.*

No one attended from Mr. Richmond's side of the family either, though this had more to do with their being industrialists from the Scottish marshes and so both too busy, and too far for a minor wedding at the other end of the country.

Some friends of William's had turned up. They sat politely in the back of the church and threw confetti as the couple left, but they seemed rather subdued in their verbal congratulations. They appeared to admire Mr Richmond for his choice of wife only in so far as it reflected a bold choice, not a wise one.

It appeared only the couple truly thought the union an uncomplicated and beautiful match but the lack of people could not crush her joy. Nora was in heaven.

The organist and Mr Brampton, the father of one of the choirboys, were witnesses. The organist had not even bothered dressing up, and signed the certificate of matrimony with an "X" having never learned in all his years of playing A-flats through G-sharps on his keyboard to read or write the letters with a pen.

Nora had stood at the front of the church and waited impatiently through the long preamble, willing time to pass faster so she could hear the words that would tie the knot, that would seal her marriage to her wonderful William. In the same breath she was willing it to run slower so that she could savour every moment of this day. The two forces of anticipation and appreciation warred within her as the priest intoned in beautifully pronounced Latin, which William had explained to her before the service.

There was a pause and the intimate group behind her all intoned, "Amen."

Nora was impatient at this arcane slowness, she was so close to the moment where they would be bound together in the eyes of God and man. She would no longer be a servant gazing up at him in subjugation, but his wife, a part of him bound in adoration.

It was too much, she kept thinking. Too much joy, too much good fortune.

She heard the phrase in Latin meaning "give this couple joy", and she could have danced, but beneath the joy a voice was screaming to make itself heard, a voice that she tried to drown out.

It already had given her joy. More joy than she had ever imagined possible. Beneath her dress, across her shoulders she felt a twinge of pain, a thin scar where Miss June's rod had broken her open. She felt that pain now as a flash of almost religious agony, a pain that made her happiness all the sweeter.

She looked to her beloved, this tall handsome man

with his dark hair and green eyes, all dressed up in his fine suit and top hat. He looked how she imagined angels must look. His face was serious as he listened along to the preacher, nodding at key points and intoning, "Amen". But he too could hardly maintain that facade of sobriety and his lips kept breaking into a smile which he then struggled to hide.

The voice continued to repeat its chant, below all the happiness she felt, this voice made explicit the misgiving that seemed like a drop of ink to cloud the clarity of her joy. That voice when it could be heard said, "This cannot last."

She refused its message and smiled. Under her veil she had none of William's need to hide her pleasure. She smiled until she felt her face might split in two.

But the voice was still there. *This cannot last.*

The priest said, in Latin, "Make their marriage a token of your love," and Nora had to wonder if it was blasphemous to think that even God could not love anything or anyone as fully as she loved William.

Finally, the moment came when they said, "I do."

The rings were slipped onto each other's fingers and William lifted her veil to place his lips firmly on hers.

The whole church melted away around her and her whole world was in the warm softness of his mouth. It was too brief and when he broke away, much to the priest's horror she pulled him back for a longer, more intense kiss, which he returned with a passion that neither could have imagined displaying before such an audience.

When they finished and the bells were rung, they left the church by the main doors, no longer individuals, but two parts of a single beautiful whole.

* * *

There was little need to stay on in Hamley-on-Thames, no family to celebrate with on her side and none willing to on his. Instead, she found herself being lifted up into a carriage by William's strong hands. They sat together in the closed-top carriage and they barely parted lips all the way to Devon.

Then it was a week in a seaside cottage, moonlit walks along the beaches which at low tide turned into stretches of what seemed like miles of shimmering sand that seemed to blend into the sea rather than mark its boundary.

The garden of the cottage was alive with bees humming back and forth between the flower beds which were in full bloom. The lambs in the field and the daily catch of eels which the locals seemed ever to be touting to them all spoke of the annual eruption of new life.

To Nora though, it was a seminal eruption... Genesis, not renewal, the beginning of something new not just for her as Mrs Richmond, but for the whole planet and above her even the stars.

It was all too much, and the voice inside her continued to chant with greater and greater power, *this cannot last.*

CHAPTER FIVE

When they first arrived at their home, Nora stood and looked up at the house of which she was now the lady. It had not changed on the outside but everything about it seemed new and different to her, coloured by this new relationship.

As she stood staring up at the house, she felt William's arm across her back, just below the scar, and his other behind her knees. Before she could work out what was about to happen, she was whisked up into the air and the house took on a horizontal slant.

She flung her arms about William's neck and sat up in his arms, kissing him on the cheek.

He was so gentle with her, it felt more like floating than being carried. In this way they drifted up the steps to the door and when Stephen opened it to them, he bore her across the threshold.

The house was utterly spotless.

Stephen, in their absence, had even stormed the walls of disorder that had built up in William's laboratories. With the Herculean efforts which he had first warned Nora would be necessary, he had brought cleanliness and a sense of the system to the rooms.

William and Nora quickly set about undoing his hard work. It seemed vital to William that he get back to work. More so now that his family appeared to be making threats about his incomes and inheritances.

He had a few patents out and had sold a method of producing red dye to a local textile magnate in return for regular dividends. But to secure his income against family meddling would take a more concerted approach to praxis over theory.

Nora threw herself more fully into William's work,

assisting by acting as his scribe, fetcher, carrier and spare set of hands whenever a particularly complex set of equipment required it.

Slowly but surely, she was learning a little natural philosophy, but she got a sense from William that he was uncomfortable with her presence in the lab in a way he had not suggested before.

Over time the voice that cried so insistently that their love and happiness could not last faded, and became only a vague shadow which would appear every now and then during the occasional nightmare.

The issue of her working came to a head a few weeks after they returned. Nora was hunched over a volume of anatomical drawings and producing cross-reference cards. They were for a series of dissections William was planning to do on some vile looking monkey fetuses that had arrived from the New World. The diagrams laid out many of the more interesting internal features of adult monkeys and William was attempting to produce a similar set of diagrams of in utero development to augment the cases of Charles Darwin who had noted the many similarities in the earliest developmental stages of most animal species.

Nora's writing was crude, but clear, and followed the lines on the page in large looping strokes. She enjoyed the feel of pen on paper, the rough resistance of the paper's texture against the flat edge of the pen's nib.

Her favourite task was collating quotations for him using endless commonplace books and concordances. Through it she began to understand the beauty of not just the words, but the ideas and stories that this natural philosophy could tell. How her love for William was part of an unbroken chain of ancestors leading back to something that could not be called human to something truly animal. It frightened her now, to look into the monkey's cage and see in the two primates there holding hands a mirror image in some way of her and William kissing in the chapel.

It is interesting to contemplate an entangled bank, clothed with many plants of many kinds, with birds singing on the bushes, with various insects flitting about, and with worms crawling through the damp earth, and to reflect that these elaborately constructed forms, so different from each other, and dependent on each other in so complex a manner, have all been produced by laws acting around us.

She had written those words down once for William. Copying them exactly, from the end of *The Origin of Species*, one of three books that seemed to most excite William. Now, as their relationship grew and her knowledge with it, she was becoming more and more intrigued by it all.

There is grandeur in this view of life, with its several powers, having been originally breathed into a few forms or into one and that, whilst this planet has gone cycling on according to the fixed law of gravity, from so simple a beginning endless forms most beautiful and most wonderful have been, and are being, evolved.

That was what William wished to illustrate with these dissections, the unity of all life that grew in wombs. She blotted the row of page numbers she had copied out and turned to the next book as she half listened to William washing his hands behind her.

Though she loved much of his work, here she was struggling to find the grandeur. It all seemed disgusting, the wet flesh of the animals, the strange forms of the unborn infants. She wondered what William would think if she were to become pregnant, what sort of experiment he might view that as.

A few moments later she felt his hand rest affectionately on her shoulder, and all those thoughts evaporated. The warmth of his hand reminding her that his curiosity was a vital human drive, something as close to their love as anything else.

Checking her hand for any ink spots first, she laid her fingers over his and continued turning the pages with her other hand.

Through their touch she felt the affection flow both ways and was reassured. Somehow, she felt that every doubt she had about William and his love, the voice that said it could not last, every part of it was rooted in the way Miss June had raised her.

With some effort she put the cold of the orphanage behind her and focused every part of her mind and soul on the warmth of William's skin on hers.

"This work is making a hunchback of you, Nora," he said. His voice was laughing, but she could tell that he was not all in jest. She put the pen down, straightened her back and turned so she could look him in the face.

"I know you hate to see me work as I did when I was your employee. But this is not the labour of a servant but of a wife. Done for love, not money."

"But it is hard work none the less. What kind of man wears his wife thin?"

"The work of the lab is not so hard, my love. I work no harder than you. And get no less joy from this process of peeling back the mask of mother nature."

This seemed to surprise him somewhat.

"What?" she asked. "You thought that men alone could enjoy puzzling out a mystery? Perhaps you should turn your microscopes on me as a specimen of the female species. We are not hothouse orchids but the self-same species as you and Mr Darwin and all the rest."

He pondered this a while. "I had not thought of you doing all this from fascination." His voice sounded apologetic."

"Nor did I at first. But the more I learn of this way of viewing the world, the more passion I feel for being part of it. I have so many questions and I love that working with you in these labs so often delivers answers, and yet, for every answer —"

"— there are a dozen new questions." His face had changed again to the one which he looked at her in moments of deep intimacy.

It is a joy, too, when one finds out some new aspect of the one you love, she reflected. Every bit as much as the joy of finding out some new fact that only God had known before yourself.

"Very well, there are so many things I want to discuss regarding these foetal dissections. Have you noticed how like gills the folds at the smaller one's neck are?"

Before she could answer there came, from the ground floor, the most almighty crashing sound.

"Good Lord!" cried William.

Nora felt a flash of fear. She had heard of gangs that broke, entered, and cut throats of those they robbed. But it was still light out, the sun only just having dipped below the artificial skyline generated by London's many brick and mortar edifices.

Surely no one would be prowling about with nefarious intent on a day like this.

It reminded her of a story she had told Valeria once when they were younger, curled up beneath the rags that passed for blankets at the orphanage.

A ghost story of her own construction that once she had told it, she was sure she had been told by the ghost itself. A frantic horrified creature whose fearsomeness came wholly from the misunderstanding of the people who witnessed it.

With their breath misting in front of them, she had spun the tale up improvising for Valeria, as the family, newly moved into a beautiful home were beset every few hours by a fearsome banging and crashing.

In the final moments, the family dogged by the house running from the ghost leaving behind a little orphan who finds that the ghost was not trying to chase the family away but to get them to help her.

The ghost did not know that it was dead. That was the real horror.

Nora could not figure out quite why this memory from so long ago came back with such clarity and force, but the crash from below was very like how she imagined the banging of the ghost.

William was looking at her with a look of worry on his face. "My God, Nora. Your pale as a ghost. I'm sure Stephen has just dropped something."

Sure enough, a few moments later she heard the familiar tapping of Stephen's feet on the stairs. No doubt bearing with him an explanation and apology for some broken vase.

Although, there did appear to be someone with him, ascending the stairs in near lockstep. Not a ghost then, most likely a clumsy delivery boy or the like.

Nora looked to William for some reassurance. He looked a little concerned, but nothing on his face suggested that she should feel as frightened as she felt. Despite that, he suggested that she go into the next room and keep an ear out for his call.

She did so, rushing quickly across the physical sciences lab and slipping into the chemical laboratory, closing the door behind her and inserting the key into the lock. Her hand hovered on the key, not yet turning it and locking it, but ready to if required.

She couldn't shake that feeling of the past reaching

up and grabbing her with a hand that felt almost physical.

The door on the other side opened and she could hear Stephen and William speaking to each other. She couldn't quite make out the words though, the door muffled all but a few words which did nothing to elaborate on what might be going on.

It certainly did not appear to be a robbery, and nothing too ghastly as a ghost. So what then? Why had William not called her back? A business meeting then?

Eventually, she heard a third voice, the owner of that ghostly pair of feet. It seemed friendly enough, a little familiar in a way that amplified that feeling of being drawn back to Miss June's and nights of storytelling with Valeria.

This was a man's voice, one that she couldn't quite put a face to. She leaned closer to the door, trying to make out the words. She thought she caught a name. But it couldn't be.

She could have sworn the voice had said... but no, it couldn't be. She pictured the starving boy who had befriended Valeria and whom Valeria had loved so much as a girl.

Could this be the same boy?

The voice might be his, it sounded about right, but it had been so long. Surely the years had changed his voice — no wonder it wasn't completely familiar. Was it really him?

The strange sense of fear of the past gave way to its opposite:

William called out for her, "My love, could you bring some tea in, three cups?"

There was pause and the mumble of obscured speech.

"And some sugar for Allen here, please."

My God, she thought. It is really him.

CHAPTER SIX

*V*aleria read to Miss Umbridge from *Federalist No. 10*. When she finished, Deloris asked her, "And what do you think on this matter, young lady?"

The old lady seemed somewhat breathless, as if excited by the prospect of debate again and a light sweat shone on her brow.

For a moment Valeria dared to hope that she would become like her mother again. That her greatest dream would come true. Only that dream was tarnished by this illness and she felt a knife edge of fear for the woman she had come to love.

Delores was in her bed, the covers drawn up to her

neck, while Valeria sat in a tall armchair by her bedside table and read the words of one of England's most successful foes.

Unsure quite what to answer to this question, Valeria paused and thought about it. She understood she was so recently out of the dog-house that she must remain careful not to give Miss Umbridge any reason to take offence.

"I think a fear of majority rule is a wise one," Valeria said cautiously. "Quite as fearsome as that of any minority rule. So, I would think that to create a fair and prosperous society..." She paused and reached about for something in her reading that might address this. "One that is fair and prosperous for all that is, one must... Well, take for example, me and you, Miss Umbridge. What if we were to flip a coin and if it came up heads we stayed in our positions and if it came up tails we were to swap? I was to own all your holdings and have sway and dominion over the household staff, of which you would then be one."

"Valeria, I believe I see where you are taking this discussion already. I do hope this is to be as impertinent as I anticipate." She coughed twice, and touched her brow, squinting a little as if suffering a headache.

"Are you all right, Miss Umbridge? Should I fetch anything for you?"

Though Cook had warned her that Delores had been vague and forgetful, Valeria had seen none of it thus far. Cook had told her that she believed Miss Umbridge was keeping a secret about her health. That she was hiding it from them all but mostly from Valeria.

"She thinks of you as a daughter," Cook said. "I know she doesn't show it but that was why she was so betrayed when that... that incident with the boy happened."

Valeria didn't know whether to be happy, proud, or scared. Why would Deloris hide something like this? A mother's secret, why would she hide something from her? At first, she worried that it was something bad about her health but then sense took over. It was because she no longer trusted her. It was to be expected and she would win that trust back.

With that thought in mind, she began to think about her interactions but Deloris had seemed just like her old self, sharp and insightful, and almost as kind as she used to be. But she did seem frail. Her hands shook when she lifted her tea and every now and again, she would lean back and lay her head on her pillows and close her eyes as if it was all too much for her.

The cough was new, and worried Valeria who had seen too many girls carried off by infections of the lungs in Miss June's home. A cough could be nothing, but it could also be the omen of another small unmarked grave and another empty place at the table. Death was so common among the young in London that even someone ensconced in the protective confines of high walls and thick pocketbooks could be struck down by something as insignificant as a cough and a fever.

Fear traced a finger down her spine as she remembered cook's words. *She thinks of you as a daughter.*

Valeria loved Delores like a mother and could not bear the thought of anything happening to her.

"No, no, child, I am quite all right," Miss Umbridge said. "Do go on. You were plotting my overthrow.

Tell me more of this gamble we are to take." There was an upward curl to her lips and her eyes shone with enjoyment.

Valeria cleared her throat for the lump of worry would not allow her words to pass.

"Well, Ma'am. The gamble is the less important part of the matter. The question that it raises is, given the gamble, how should you choose to arrange your household? If you do not know if you are to be the lady of the house or the maid then you must build a society where you would be as happy to be either."

"I see, but we are not likely to take this gamble today, are we?" Deloris asked with a chuckle. The laughter gave way to a cough, it was a little more persistent and she seemed to have some trouble clearing her throat.

Valeria took the opportunity offered by the pause. "No. We are not to take this gamble ourselves. But every child born into our society flips just such a coin. Some are born to the manor, some to the gutter and some to every gradation between. Perhaps if we worried about the people of the future in this way, we might treat those who are alive today a little better."

"A fine rhetorical argument, Valeria. You have learned much from your study of Cicero and Socrates. I feel that few people could have gained what you have from scouring my bookshelves. However…"

Valeria couldn't stop herself from interrupting. "On the contrary, Miss Umbridge. Books like this…" She held up the book. "Books that no one of my birth could have accessed but for the generosity of those who can afford to keep such a library — these would benefit all who read them every bit as much as I."

The smile remained on Miss Umbridge's features. The older lady liked to be challenged and she nodded.

"— it is the idea of Darwin that each generation draws from the one before," Miss Umbridge said and Valeria listened respectfully, because she understood that the coin would forever go unflipped.

"No coin is flipped concerning character. The ruling class, even in a democracy like ours, must be drawn from those qualified by the success in ruling of their ancestors. We all have our place in society. The unread and unwashed masses cannot be expected to rule, any more than an old lady like me could be expected to push a plough..."

She coughed again and winced.

Valeria leaned forward, worry clouding over the arguments she was preparing in her mind against this hybridised vision of Darwin and Burke that Miss Umbridge had synthesised. The old lady did not look well, the sweat was no longer a light sheen on her forehead but was forming droplets on her nose and running down her brow in rivulets.

"You look most unwell, Miss Umbridge. Are you sure I can't fetch you a brandy or call for your physician? Could I at least—"

Valeria stopped dead midsentence as Miss Umbridge coughed again and again into her handkerchief. Even before she drew the cloth away from her mouth, Valeria could see the bright speckling of red blood droplets standing out like signal lights against the yellow of the old lady's spittle.

This looked bad. A bloodied cough could mean a tubercular infection.

"Yes. Maybe that would be best, Valeria... I forgive you for you have been like a daughter to me."

"Thank you," Valeria said but she could say no more for the tears that filled her eyes.

As the old woman pronounced this, her head slumped forwards for a moment, she looked dizzy and confused. Her next words sounded slurred, as if she were just woken from a deep sleep and had not yet worked out whether she was truly awake yet.

"Coul...d you have... C...c...c... cook go for a doctor." On the final word she faded out to the barest of whispers and began to cough again.

Valeria stood up, unsure of what to do; the room seemed small and hot, and everything seemed very far away. Her stomach churned with worry. She was terrified to leave the old woman alone, but Cook wouldn't be in the pantry where the bell pull would ring.

Pull yourself together, Valeria snapped to herself. She tried to clear her mind, to think clearly. What needed doing? First thing was to go now and find Cook and send her out to fetch the Doctor. After that she could return and tend to her old friend.

With immense effort she tore her walleyed stare away from Miss Umbridge's coughing fit. She quickly checked that Deloris was comfortable and then rushed from the room. Taking the stairs three at a time she rushed down in such a flurry it felt almost as if she was falling rather than running down them.

In the kitchen she found Cook. She was cutting onions, and her eyes were streaming with tears from the fumes.

"Nothing sadder than a chopped onion," she joked turning to face Valeria.

If Valeria was unsure about how Miss Umbridge's illness was affecting her she had no doubt when she saw how Cook reacted to her face.

She laid the second onion down only half-diced and put a hand to her heart.

"What in God's name, child? Are you all right?"

"Yes, Cookie. I am fine, it is Miss Umbridge, she's not well.

It took a few runs at the explanation to get Cookie to understand. The words seemed to rush out of Valeria in the wrong order and then she would stumble trying to fit them back together trying again and stumbling over them once more.

Eventually she managed to get it out. "She's coughing up blood and... and there's something else wrong. I don't know what. She won't talk properly. It's like she's not fully awake. Please, Cook, fetch Doctor Strathairn as fast as you can."

Cookie immediately mixed a glass of brandy and water, a strong one for Valeria and a weak one for Miss Umbridge. To Miss Umbridge's she added a few drops of laudanum and once Valeria had swallowed hers, she sent her up to Miss Umbridge with the other glass.

As Valeria left the kitchen Cook was putting on her hat and heading for the door.

When Valeria arrived back in Miss Umbridge's room, the situation was much worse than it had been just a few minutes before. Miss Umbridge was slumped forward. Her head was almost in her own lap and she seemed to be trying and failing to murmur something to the bedsheets which the bedsheets, and Valeria, were stubbornly refusing to understand.

Valeria carefully helped Miss Umbridge to sit back in her bed, leaning her against the headboard of her bed and putting several pillows behind her neck.

The old lady looked wrong, her face was the wrong shape or something, it was hard to pin down, some subtle change had come over her. As with the meeting with Allen when the years had brought about changes to a once familiar face, to her it seemed illness had done in minutes what it took age many years to resolve.

The old lady coughed once more and then appeared to fall completely silent. Her chest wasn't moving.

Valeria panicked, thinking Miss Umbridge was dead, she leaned forward, pressing her ear against the woman's chest. Valeria could just make out the thudding of her heart, faint and fast, then the old lady drew a rattly breath and coughed again and Valeria sighed with relief.

Sick was bad, but better by far than the fear of death.

Miss Umbridge tried to say something, but the words were wrong, slurred beyond all recognition. Some spittle ran down the right corner of her mouth which sagged monstrously.

Valeria was terrified, she had never seen anything like this.

The old lady's entire right side had collapsed. Her right arm lay limp on the bedsheets while her other arm tried to reach out to Valeria. Her right eye was almost closed and her eyebrow sagged. It was as if she had been punctured and the air let out of half of her. It looked monstrous and she realised that the beginning of this process was what had given the old lady her strange and alien air.

"It'll be all right, Ma'am," Valeria kept saying. "It will be all right."

Though, she could not imagine how it possibly could be all right. Whatever had struck down Miss Umbridge had happened fast, and had broken her in a way that seemed hideous to look at and fearful to contemplate.

Valeria sat by her side, repeating her one line. "It is going to be all right. It will be all right. Don't worry now. It will all be all right."

In her heart she knew it would not, could not be all right.

THE MOTHER'S SECRET

The doctor seemed to take forever to arrive, immediately dismissing Valeria and Cookie to wait in the corridor outside while he conducted whatever tests the medical establishment demanded of such symptoms.

Valeria felt useless. So rather than waiting for the doctor she headed for the library. pulling down whatever she could find in the medical section. It was too much information for her to sift through, but she tried. Hunting through indexes and contents lists to see if she could find the trouble. She had little hope that this would add anything that the doctor might not already have worked out, but it kept her mind busy searching and researching rather than simply worrying about her old friend.

She had made some progress, identifying the symptoms as apoplexy or a stroke. What she read was not encouraging. Paralysis, confusion, death, and all right at the same moment that Miss Umbridge and Valeria were just beginning to build back some sort of trust.

It was not fair, she thought. Each time something appeared to finally set things right in her world, something else countered by shattering it. Escaping

Miss June's and losing Nora, Allen's return to her and his betrayal of her, and now as that seemed to be on the verge of being mended this plethora, or as Galen would have it, a blockage of the "animal spirit" in the brain, might end Valeria's role in this house altogether.

When, eventually, she heard the doctor leave Miss Umbridge's room and speak to Cookie Valeria dashed upstairs to hear what he had to say.

Sure enough, his diagnosis was a stroke, just as her reading had suggested. His prognosis was more optimistic than the writers she had read. Although, according to him there was little to do but keep an eye on the old lady and hope that time would heal this wound as it does so many.

"Sometimes the paralysis passes over time," he said. "Some people remain paralysed until their deaths. For now, though, it is impossible to say what her prognosis is. I will check in with her tomorrow. In the meantime, you will need to keep close observations of her. You must also take care of her every function, she will not be able to wash herself or get herself to the water closet. You will need to assist her in all these things. You should also notify Mr

Wright as he is her executor in all matters and she will be unable to manage her concerns in her current state. Is that all quite clear?"

Once he had established that Valeria and Cookie were clear on all the implications and necessary undertakings, he left his bill, some laudanum to help with any pain, and then the house.

CHAPTER SEVEN

The angry looking man followed Allen upstairs through glittering halls.

Allen couldn't help but notice the sterling silver frames on the wall, the gold-plated chandelier in the hallway, and the elegant candlesticks. For these he was sure he could get sixpence each from a fence he knew down Cheapside.

Even as this passed through his mind, he found he did not really expect to escape. He was tired. Physically and also deep within his soul. He was not looking for a moment to make a break, but instead, walking up the stairs ahead of this old man and feeling almost grateful that it would all be coming to an end one way or another.

On the landing he paused and the man came up behind him, blocking off his only escape route. Without saying a word, the man gestured to the first door on the left and Allen took the cold doorknob in a firm grasp and turned.

He smiled a little to himself, his first smile in months. At last there was to be some sort of resolution to the nagging pain of living. He would be hung by the law, returned to Taylor to be killed or worse, it didn't matter. He no longer had to run.

The room he entered was a riot of things worth stealing. Shining polished brass everywhere, every bit of it connected or housing some expensive, precision machine. There were half a dozen sea chronometers whose price alone Allen eyeballed as being worth a shilling a piece to a fence at the barest of minimums. That did not account for the telescopes and microscopes, barometers, voltmeters, and some sort of hand-cranked machine with an array of coiled wires inside. The books too would be worth a pretty penny.

In fact, the room was so full of riches that it took him a little while to realise that he was being inspected by a face that a moment ago had been inspecting microbes beneath a lens.

"Well, Stephen, who is our guest?" asked the inspecting face. Allen noted it was a face that Valeria would have described as *most comely* now that she had been reading so many books.

The old man, who must therefore be Stephen, answered the face. "I have yet to inquire as to his name or occupation. Our introduction was a little brusque."

"Did this have anything to do with that almighty crash or indeed the carrying ons in the street a moment ago?"

"Yes, Sir. He came into the living room by way of the front window. Very luckily for him I had opened it to give the room an airing. He still managed to do some damage to your chess table."

"I see," the inquisitive face now took on a look of deep pondering. "Never mind, Stephen. I was never much a one for chess. No talent for it. Now, young Sir. Your turn. You'd best give us an account of yourself. Were you here for our silverware, or simply escaping the hounds?"

Allen took a moment to assess his options. There was an obvious answer, but the two men seemed so genial and friendly that he could expect nothing but a trap in their behaviours. Taylor would do the same thing, go all friendly when you were expecting a clipped ear. It made one cautious of tones like this.

"Well," he began. "I can assure you, Sir, that I am not here to pilfer your valuables. There was a misunderstanding. I gave a flower to a young lady, whose father — and fiancée — saw the romantic act of a foolish urchin as a threat upon the lady's virtue and saw fit to deliver a whipping to my very person. I apologise for having violated your privacy, and damaging your property. It was an act of self-preservation."

It was a story worthy of Nora, even the stilted language of her fictions had made their way into the tale he told. He was rather proud.

"An urchin, you say. That seems a bit of a stretching of the truth. You look to be what? Sixteen, maybe. Seventeen, even. A man."

The compliment gave Allen a brief flash of pride,

which he quickly tempered. If this was a trap, he must be careful not to be lured into it.

"Well, I hope you won't mind my having Stephen check your tale out with the gentlemen out in the street. Discretely of course. In the meantime, I will have Mrs Richmond fetch us some tea. Will you join me? I'm Mr Richmond, and you are?"

This seemed hopeful, with this Stephen character outside and this gentleman whose naive pally-ness seemed no act at all. "I'm Allen, Sir. Just Allen."

Mr Richmond smiled broadly and rapped on the door. "My love, could you bring some tea in, three cups. Tell me, Allen, do you take sugar in your tea?"

"Yes, please, Sir."

"And bring some sugar for our guest please."

The voice that responded sounded oddly familiar, though muffled as it was by the walls, and the strange noises of the house — which appeared to be hiding a menagerie and an aviary within its walls — he wasn't quite able to work out what it was that seemed so familiar.

Mr Richmond made a little small talk, showing off

some of the instruments of science with which the room was full and, in a few moments, Mrs Richmond arrived back with the tea.

Allen's jaw dropped. It was Nora. Valeria's closest friend in that God forsaken pit that Miss June had run. "Nora."

"Good evening, Allen," she said.

"Well, how do you like that?" said Allen. "'Good evening, Allen,' she says, like its nothing. Like this isn't the second strangest coincidence of my entire life. And you, the wife of a regular gent?"

The world seemed to have taken on a cant, everything lopsided and confused. How on earth had all this come to pass?

"I fear I must have hit my head on that window a little too hard, Mr Richmond. Because Mrs Richmond here appears to be an old acquaintance who I thought I would never see again in my life, London being so great a metropolis. But here I am either imagining the impossible or witness to it."

"You imagine nothing, Allen." She was smiling,

clearly enjoying his astonishment, and doing well at hiding her own. "It really is me... Nora."

He turned to Mr Richmond. "Well, Sir. This is remarkable."

"Yes," said Mr Richmond, his face painted in all the usual shapes of bemusement. "Remarkable, as you remarked. Nora, how on earth do you know this young man?"

Allen stood on as Nora poured the tea and told the tale of Valeria and his friendship. The night Valeria had sneaked him past Miss June and fed him soup she had saved from her own portion. Of the little blonde rascal that had caught them and brought Miss June down upon them, and finally of his flight, and disappearance from their lives.

It was strange to hear that familiar story of his childhood explained and portrayed from the standpoint of someone other than himself. He and Valeria had recounted the tale in the exchange of conversation, but to have a full story with a beginning, middle and end spun about him was a strange experience.

Nora's telling of the tale seemed to arrange the

haphazard events of those long past days into a kind of logical order with events happening, not in the jumble of sensations and emotions that he had experienced, but with the cold clarity and order of a ghost story told about a campfire, or a bawdy joke.

When she was done, she turned to him. He gazed back at her, examining the beautiful, deep pools of her eyes. "What happened next?" she asked.

"Yes," Mr Richmond asked. "What does chapter two of this tale look like."

Allen pondered this for a while. Considering the wisest tale to spin for these rich fools, how best to leverage this into something he could use to get in better with Taylor. Maybe get back to regular food rations and a bed closer to the fire in the gang's current accommodations.

But instead, he looked into Nora's eyes. Seeing how happy she was. He could hardly recognise the cowed and fearful little girl he'd known in the face of this woman.

So instead of lying, or trying to find his way into their good books he made a full confession. He told them about the years of stealing on the streets. The work with Abel. Finding Valeria and betraying Valeria. He talked and talked, telling the whole truth. It came out in scattered order, nothing like as clear as Nora's account, but it bridged the gap between her tale and the now they all shared.

He even told the truth, correcting the lie of how he came to be in their drawing room.

Mr Richmond's kind smile did not fade as he told his tale. In fact, the story of criminality, of victimisation and of victimising appeared to do nothing to extinguish either of the couple's human warmth towards him.

Eventually he reached the end and fell silent.

Mr Richmond, who had been leaning forward, leaned back then. He threw his head back and looked up at the ceiling, taking a moment, Allen thought, to assess all that he had just heard. Allen could almost hear the debate as to whether or not to call the police, to have Stephen bring the men in from the street so justice could be done.

It was Nora who broke the silence in the end.

"Well," she said. "We cannot send you back to this

Mr Taylor. We have plenty of room here. You must stay until we can work out what best to do with you."

"Yes," Mr Richmond said. He suddenly seemed very pleased. Clearly, he had made up his mind of what to make of Allen's tale. "I know just what to do with you. I need someone to assist in the labs, and to take on the physical work that worries my heart when Nora does it."

Nora seemed about to object.

"Now, Nora. I don't mean to take you out of the labs. But this will free you up to do more of the mental labour involved in our work."

Allen noted he put a special emphasis on the word "our", and that Nora appeared to react very strongly to this word. Something had clearly passed between the couple but Allen could not tell if it were good or bad. Just that it mattered a great deal to Nora what Mr Richmond had just said.

It took a moment for the offer to sink in. Employment, room, board, in this house with his friend Nora and under the protection of the upper-class she'd married into. It was too good to believe. This much luck did not fall into a man's lap without exacting a heavy price. But exactly what the price would be he couldn't work out. That made him much afeared.

He looked at Nora again. Perhaps it was not as he feared. Perhaps she was making an offer out of nothing but kindness. Perhaps, just perhaps, a corner had been turned and he could make a new life, here, out from under the shadow of Abel Taylor, somewhere that felt safe, somewhere he might come to see as a home.

He wouldn't mind earning steady pay once again. He couldn't remember the last time he'd been a salaried worker. Perhaps back when he was a shoeshine boy. It had been two or perhaps three years or maybe more. Time passed strangely when you were hungry and desperate.

His eyes stung and he awkwardly wiped away the tears that seemed to have formed in them. He didn't say "yes". Somehow it didn't seem enough. Instead, he kept repeating, "Thank you." To the two of them.

The tears began to flow freely, and for once they were not of sorrow, but of joy.

CHAPTER EIGHT

*V*aleria waited in the corridor, anxiously biting her nails as the doctor went about his weekly checkup with Miss Umbridge. Every week he would return and pass judgement on whether she was closer to death or closer to a return to her old life — or as had been the case the last three times he had called, whether she remained locked in the living death she inhabited now.

It had been weeks since the stroke and although Deloris had held on, and in fact seemed to be out of danger, she still was unable to speak more than a few badly slurred words at a time. She struggled with her breathing and left her bed only under the assisted power of both Cook and Valeria.

Thomas had moved into a spare bedroom and had immediately set about taking control of the house. He viewed many of Miss Umbridge's old habits with the staff as *grossly inefficient* and so spent much of his time scolding them and ordering them into new habits. Cook's menus rarely went unedited by his scathing remarks and the other domestic staff were subject to the most caustic and bitter chastisements.

Gone was the man who would talk to Cookie as if they were equals. He had become a puritan, berating the staff for no other reason than he could. It seemed that he despised any joy they may feel.

Valeria was often the receiver of his most brutal judgement. She had been commanded more times than she could count to redo some chore. Not because it was done badly but because it had been done in a manner different to what Mr Wright liked.

That very morning, she had been forced to reclean all the windows in Miss Umbridge's study because she had cleaned the windows with clockwise circles of the paper and not, as Mr Wright preferred, counter-clockwise. It hurt her that he spent so much time in her study. It had always been a place filled with good memories... they were turning to ash now that he spent most of his days there.

All the time she could feel his eyes studying the movement of her legs and buttocks behind the curtain of her dress. She suspected the extra time was only a bonus to him now. His real joy seemed to be in his elevation to petty dictator of the house. Once he was one of the staff, just like her, now he had power over them and he relished it.

She did her best to avoid him, but wherever she went, there he would be soon after she arrived. His hungry eyes tracking her every movement and his pompous voice telling her again and again her many faults imagined and real.

As she was stood there, waiting for the doctor's prognosis, Cook came up behind her.

"Miss Valeria," she said, her voice coloured with the peevishness she always had when she had just been spoken to by Mr Wright. "The *master* wants to see you in *his* office." She managed to wring from the word's "master" and "his" every possible drop of sarcasm.

Valeria's heart sank. She loathed being alone with the man.

With heavy steps she slowly left Miss Umbridge behind and mounted the stairs to what now appeared to be Mr Wright's office.

As she entered, she found him sat looking smarmy and self-satisfied. A cigar in his hand was burning with a sinister red glow and filled the room with a foul, oily stink.

"Valeria," he said. "You look miserable, oppressed even. Despite Miss Umbridge, and of course, my own generosity. You never fail to look like the downtrodden servant. I too served, but was never servile the way you are."

Valeria nodded to quietly acknowledge the insult, knowing that to argue would be to provoke reprisals.

"But I have the perfect fix for your state, the ideal way to elevate you and pull you up out of the squalor that you seem to cultivate within yourself."

She continued to stare at the floor and silently hate this man as he continued.

"I am now well established in my profession. My

business interests are flourishing and I am now turning to other aspects of my life. I find myself wondering how best to complete the plan God has for the lives of men like me. I look at my home and see a place that is warm, but clearly that of a bachelor. It is time I think to bring a little feminine brightness into my home. And so, I have been looking about for a wife."

Surely not, thought Valeria. He can't possibly think I would ever...

"I have settled upon you, Valeria. I see potential beneath your flaws. This is why I am far tougher on you than on those who have no chance of improvement, like Cookie. You could, under my close tutelage, be a fine wife, and I wish to give you the opportunity to become something more than you are — no longer an orphan scullery maid, but a gentleman's wife."

"You are no gentleman," Valeria said fiercely.

For a moment there was total silence, as if Mr Wright were unable to believe what he had just heard.

"What did you say?" was his eventual response.

"I said you are no gentleman. You are a petty, cruel, and weak man. You curry favour with those you fear and bear contempt for those over whom society has given you power. You are a pathetic man, with no inner life or moral character. I would not... I could never... never marry you. Would never be so mercenary an animal as to debase myself to be your wife. I may be an orphan, but there is no position lower than to be a member of your household. You have come into my home and parasitized the resources of my mistress, but you will never have me, can never have me."

There was a long silence while he composed himself. His smug smile had vanished and been replaced first by a look of horror and now by a furious anger. He stubbed his cigar out with a violent gesture of his hand.

"You dare speak to me like this?" he snarled.

"I do."

"I am in charge of this household, as Miss Umbridge's executor. She may have been willing to forgive the thief you allowed into her home. But I do not. You may leave now, or you may remain until the police arrive to try you for trespassing and conspiracy to rob this house. This house is not your home, will never be your home. Get out. Now."

Valeria said nothing, but turned and walked out.

It would do no good with this man, she knew, to beg or plead. She could not bring before him the friendship she and Miss Umbridge had once had. The fact that she had thought of her as a daughter. No one had heard it and no one would believe her. Nor could she expect him to pay much mind to the many hours a day she spent carrying the old lady to the bath. Or lifting her to place a chamber pot beneath her. Or the messy process of cleaning Miss Umbridge up afterwards.

The other maids had helped, but Valeria had done the brunt of it. She wished to look after her benefactor and the woman she had come to care for. The woman who had been the closest thing she had to a mother. The other girls were more than happy to avoid these more difficult jobs.

Mr Wright continued to speak, denouncing her foolishness and telling her what a rise in the world she was turning down, but she was no longer listening to his vapid platitudes. In the end her struggle had not been with the upper class as her book had said, but with the petty middle rungs that scrabbled for position in the gap between the haves like Miss Umbridge and the have nots below them.

Valeria walked down the stairs, with a kind of dream-like calm, and without even stopping to pick up her coat she walked straight out the front door and into the cold wind which scoured the street. She was leaving her home... her mother in the care of this man... but she had no choice.

CHAPTER NINE

William staggered back in from the street in considerable pain, the lump where he'd been struck was swelling alarmingly. The throbbing agony of the bruise seemed to match the regular bursts of glimmering stars that exploded in his vision with each pulse of his heart. For a moment he worried that his brain might have in some way been crushed, but it soon became clear that the affliction was *commotio cerebri* and not full brain damage.

It would be hard to keep this injury hidden from Nora.

Now that he was back in the safety of his own home, that pulsing began to slow a little as his heart beat a little less frantically. He was able to think less about the fear that he was still being pursued and more about the feeling of irritation that came from being thwarted in his plan when he had come so close to his goal.

And he *had* been so close, despite all the doubts of Inspector Lamond he had almost lured this Taylor fellow out into the open where the coppers might finally put shackles on his wrists and send him to the dock.

Instead, he had been cold-cocked by some thug wielding what might have been a black-jack, but felt like a sledgehammer to William. If Inspector Lamond hadn't been with him who knows how much nastier it could have got. Taylor had clearly brought a few extra men and it was all Lamond could do to get the pair of them out of there unscathed. Or in William's case, without further scathing.

Lamond had put a Black Maria on the street corner with half a dozen Peelers in it but they had been all but useless so fast had everything fallen apart. Taylor might not have even been there. In the morning he would have to return to the butcher's shop and give his contact a talking to, assuming he was still there.

With shaky steps William headed for the servant's quarters, feeling his way through the dark and the pain, not lighting a lamp lest he wake Nora up. The last thing she needed to know was that his attempt to help Allen had got him into real danger. She would only worry more.

He knocked on Allen's door, whispering as loudly as he dared through it. "Allen, light a candle and get out here."

A moment later a glow appeared from the crack under the door and Allen opened up, wearing a nightgown that made him look like a ghost William had seen in a book as a child.

"Good Lord, Sir," Allen said. "What in the blazes happened to you?"

"That is what I am hoping you might help me to figure out. Help me to the kitchen and pour us some brandies. Then, and only then, I'll give you the full length and breadth of the tale."

The kitchen was warm and cosy, and a few minutes later they were each beneath a blanket. They sat huddled before the hot stove in the tall wooden chairs that would normally be about the servant's dining table. Each of the two men had their hands curled about a large snifter in which a generous portion of brandy was warming.

"So, tell me, Sir. What nocturnal adventures are you engaged in? If you are carrying on with another woman, I'll have you know I won't stand for you treating Nora that way."

"It does you credit to say so, Allen. I have, in fact, been engaged with a rather different matter. It was my intention to bring this Taylor of yours to the law and hopefully clear some of the danger that stalks this city's streets for you. It was meant to be my way of a repayment for the hard work you have been doing for me. It came, quite possibly, from a rather misplaced sense of adventure."

"That's a rough crowd if you don't mind me saying, Sir. Don't you go getting more hurt... stirring them like a wasp nest."

"I won't take any more risks, not at all, Allen. In fact, I should have realised this rather sooner, and come to you for some insight. I felt that being well read would stand in for real experience dealing with these types. Instead, one of Taylor's gang taught me exactly how tough this opposition is. And he teaches the hard way. Or perhaps I should rather say the hard way wrapped in just enough leather to keep the hard way from splitting my skull clean open." William was still nursing the lump on his head.

"You are doing well for a man who got hit by a blackjack. If I can offer any help, I will."

"Thank you. I would also appreciate you making no mention of the dangerous aspects of this matter to Nora. I do not wish to worry her. I have ample backup from the Metropolitan Police Force and I will be avoiding such frontline activities as I have engaged myself in so far. The hunting of a criminal does not bear quite the comparison with hunting foxes as I hoped."

"I doubt the foxes would fight back," Allen said with a quizzical gaze.

"That is too true."

William sipped his brandy and felt the blessed heat sink into his stomach where it sent out little fingers of warmth. The pain in his head had subsided a bit and he was less oppressed by the matter now that he had shared his concerns with someone.

"The old hideout you told me about has been cleared out," William said. "Where else might we begin searching for him? Through the police and extensive bribery I have discovered any number of fences and associates but we cannot keep watch on his entire network all at once. He may be the great villain in our lives but the coppers have far more to keep on top of than just our Mr Taylor."

"Well, if he caught you in a trap-counter-trap then we might assume he is tracking you just as you tracked him. You don't look as if you were at your most cautious in your return here which means he may have one of his close associates outside this house right now."

"Good Lord, what about Stephen and Nora?!" Fear gripped William's heart. What had he done, led them right to his nest and his most precious eggs?

"Not to worry, Sir. He'll want information on his wealthy antagonist, and to be sure there isn't some mileage in blackmail or robbery before he tries anything violent. More importantly for us though, if he has a man reporting on you, then that man must find him out to make those reports. There's no better way to find where his new boarding house might be set up than to follow him back to it."

"You are a canny young fellow, aren't you, Allen?"

"Aye, Sir. I learned a thing or two from old Abel before I fell from his good graces."

"Well, you might take a little time off from your duties in the lab over the next few days to keep a wary eye out for any watchers watching the watchers from the street."

William smiled to himself, and drained his brandy. Perhaps this evening had not been the complete loss he expected.

CHAPTER TEN

Nora walked happily through the market with William's arm looped through hers and her head resting on his shoulder. They were not going anywhere in particular. William would frequently disappear for long walks through the highways and byways of London allowing his thoughts to wander. He believed one could think more creatively on a walk, hammering down the more precise and logical aspects of philosophical thought on return to the labs.

Since Nora was now assisting him in the labs, she would also now frequently accompany him on these walks. They would walk for hours, sometimes in silence, sometimes talking so much they only paused for breath when the other spoke.

Today their talk was idle, jumping about in ways more meandering even than their route which was taking them through the market district.

William was singing Allen's praises, immensely pleased with his practical knowledge, quick wits, and willingness to work long hours for his room and board.

"No matter how hard I work him, the boy seems nothing but grateful."

Nora smiled quietly to herself. Her husband would never really understand the particular way those at the bottom... those pushed outside society suffered. She understood the desperation and fear that came from being utterly powerless before a system that cared not a jot for you. Men like William, whose wealth put him beyond such worries could not understand. The money gave him an implicit power that he could never see himself any more than she could see the air around her.

"He has been of such great assistance," William

continued. "I have been trying to assist in dealing with this taskmaster of his. Although, it has been rather difficult to get the police around to my way of thinking on the subject. I've bypassed them, slipping some coin to the odd individual who seemed well placed to give me some information. I think I'm getting close to finding this Taylor chap who has treated Allen so badly. There is much less honour among thieves than even the most cynical of people might have expected. The first flash of silver will normally give up some hideaway, or contact."

This plan of William's worried Nora. It had already put him in contact with the type of person who seemed to make Allen nervous. William however, appeared oblivious to the danger. He carried a stick and the expectation of every high-born Englishman that those below him on the rungs of society would pay him the deference he deserved. The result was not so much bravery as foolishness and Nora worried that his blasé approach to this investigation would land him in real trouble. Despite her imploring him to be cautious, he continued to insist that there was no danger.

"I have been so worried by your involvement in this," Nora said. "I am sure I have seen the same man watching the house from across the street several times in the last few days."

She saw something flicker across his face.

"Not to worry, Nora. I'm sure it is nothing sinister. I am not putting myself in any danger. Only aiding the police by crossing a few informants' hands with silver. We are all perfectly safe."

They were approaching a butcher's shop when William let go of her arm. "Would you wait a moment here, Nora," he said. "I just need to have a quick word with this butcher about the last order. Stephen believes he has been shortchanging us."

Nora let him go with a look of confusion on her face. She was pretty sure the butcher's which was Stephen's preferred emporium for keeping the house supplied with meat was across the river from here. However, William would know, he had been running the house longer than she had.

While he ducked inside Nora's attention was taken by a young beggar woman who was being chased away from the door of a nearby public house by a burly looking landlord with a leering face.

A flash of pity filled Nora's heart. She remembered being cold and hungry in the orphanage too well. She would never look down on any person in hard circumstances. Without a thought, she crossed the street to where the young woman was leaning against a lamppost appearing to catch her breath between sobbing quietly.

Nora fished a silver shilling from her purse and arriving at the young woman's side, pressed the coin into her hand.

"Get yourself something to eat and a roof for the night, Miss," she said tenderly then turned back to return to the butcher's.

"Nora?"

Nora froze.

It couldn't be, she thought.

"Valeria?"

She turned once more and sure enough, the young woman looking at her from beside the lamppost was her beloved friend and companion of all those years.

The two women stood silently looking at each other,

tears of joy in their eyes. Then without a word they fell into each other's embrace.

"Oh, I have missed you," Nora finally said to Valeria.

"I have missed you too."

"How long has it been?"

"Far, far, far too long."

"An eternity. But how have you found yourself begging like this, Valeria? What happened to your position with that woman?"

At this Valeria began to cry again, and was quite inconsolable for several minutes. Eventually, she heaved a sob up out of her lungs and stopped. "She became like a mother to me... had even talked to me as if I were her daughter, but she kept a secret. One that she was terribly sick. When she succumbed to the terrible disease, the man who took over her household, until she might be well again was a monstrous sinner. He begged me to marry him that he might have his lascivious way without consequence and when I refused, he cast me out onto the street."

"Oh, my poor dear friend."

"I was a terrible fool. I took nothing with me. Not my coat or what little pay I had put aside. When I returned for them even my friends in the house turned me away and told me Mr Wright had taken everything from my room as pay for monies stolen from the house many months ago by —" At this she broke off and began to sob again.

William joined them a little later and with his usual kindness of heart immediately insisted Valeria come home with them without her even raising it with him herself.

"You, Darling Man. I am going to end up filling your house with my strays."

"It is your house now, as much as mine, my love."

"Oh, Valeria," said Nora. "We have such a surprise for you when you get home with us. You will not believe who has come to live with us."

Valeria walked between them, one arm in Nora's the other in William's. William talked ever so kindly to her on their way to her new home, and Nora felt so much love for the kindness in his soul.

Eventually, they turned off Baker Street and made it home.

How wonderful, thought Nora. *To have Allen and Valeria all together under her own roof. Everything was going to be perfect.*

CHAPTER ELEVEN

*V*aleria could hardly believe her luck. After all those months of worrying about what might have become of Nora, and now it appeared she was the lady of a fine house. The wife to a wealthy gentleman, and looking happier than Valeria ever imagined a person could be.

She felt a great deal of shame at her own appearance, though far more before Nora's handsome husband than before her friend. After all, though Nora was now a fine lady, they had been children together, sneaking what bread they could from Miss June and sharing it between them.

Her love for Nora was only challenged by her love for the house when they finally arrived. It had been weeks since she had been back inside the warmth of a house like this.

Nora immediately began fussing. An old angry looking man was asked to draw a bath for her and Nora took her up to a beautiful bedroom where she sat Valeria down.

Valeria watched as Nora began bustling about, laying out a fresh set of stays, stockings, and pinafores on the bed, then selecting an elegant but simple grey wool dress. There was something motherly in her movements. Valeria had that same strange feeling of having stepped across a vast gulf in time that she had when she had seen Allen, holding her purse, for the first time in that market.

Nora was constantly talking, telling the whole story that bridged their gap in time. How she had suffered in the orphanage — Valeria felt a deep pang of guilt. It had been hard for her to visit the orphanage, but when she had, Nora had told her all was well. She should have known better, should not have abandoned her friend there. Nora continued to tell the tale of how William had rescued her, first as a maid, and then as his wife.

Valeria smiled to herself, and listened to her friend, too overwhelmed to contribute much.

"Now," said Nora. "Once you've had a bath and changed into these clothes, come downstairs. We'll have some food and I will show you the most incredible surprise."

Nora showed her into the next room where a copper bathtub had been filled with warm water and there was fresh soap put on the rack beside it.

Then Nora went downstairs and Valeria undressed and stepped into the warmth of the water. As she scrubbed herself clean, she felt the cares of the last few weeks wash away too. The fear for Miss Umbridge, the bitter unfairness of Allen's betrayal and Mr Wright's lechery, the cold and hunger of the weeks on the street. It all seemed, for a quiet moment, to drift away from her and into the warmth of the surrounding water.

When she finally stepped out of the water she felt like a new woman. She dried herself on the softest towel she had ever felt and returned to Nora's bedroom.

The clean clothes were luxurious, the stitching on

the corset alone must have cost a month of Valeria's old wages when she worked in Miss Umbridge's house. Nora had clearly done well for herself.

A faint pang of frustration rose in her. Much of her reading had led her to resent the fact that there was little opportunity for advancement for her sex but by marrying up in the world as Nora had done.

She used one of Nora's brushes and pins to rearrange her wet hair into something acceptable for company than she went downstairs.

She followed the sound of conversation to the parlour where Nora, her husband, and the angry old man servant were seated about a coffee table.

Nora looked up at her with a beaming smile.

With them was a sight she could hardly believe.

Nora's smile faded.

"You... you thief!" Valeria screamed. With every ounce of strength she had, she threw herself at Allen who was sat with the group, a smile on his face that seemed to mock her. She reached out to claw at his eyes, screaming every filthy word she could think of at him.

"It is your fault. Every part of this. It is all your fault."

Allen had shot over the back of his chair like a rat up a drainpipe. Nora leaped across the coffee table spilling tea and cake everywhere and got between them before Valeria could get her hands-on Allen.

A moment later, Stephen and William were holding her tight while Nora tried to ask Valeria to calm down over the sound of her raging screams.

Finally, her anger subsided and she was left with a cold hollow feeling inside. All that sorrow that seemed to have come off in the bath was clinging to her again.

"I was happy until I tried to help him," she said to Nora. "He betrayed me and destroyed all the joy I had in my old home. I was cast out onto the street in part for what he did, and denied my rightful pay entirely because of his treachery."

"What on earth do you mean?" Nora asked. "What happened?" There was a pause, then to Valeria's surprise she said, "Was this after the robbery?"

"You knew about what he did to me, Nora? And you

brought him into your home? You keep him here, and parade him before me? The architect of all my sorrows?"

"Now, Valeria. There is more to the story than that," Nora said. "He did what he did to protect you from worse, and this Mr Wright of yours must bear some if not most of the blame for your fall. Now, come with me and we will speak together as women. If you still don't wish to speak to Allen ever again, we will arrange you shelter under another roof. But I think when you understand what each of you have been through you will be able to find peace between you once more."

Nora led her out and into the kitchen where she put the kettle on the hob, and cut a new slice of cake for Valeria. When all this was served up and Valeria was enjoying the first sweet mouthful of cake, Nora began.

* * *

It felt like being back in the orphanage. Nora still had that way of spinning a yarn. She told of Allen's arrival via the window, and of his travails with

Taylor. She also filled Valeria in on the hunt her husband was pursuing and her worry over it.

Then it was Valeria's turn to tell all that had happened. Of how happy she had been and how she was starting to feel like she had a home until Allen destroyed it. Then she spoke of Miss Umbridge's illness and the worry it caused and how Mr Wright had destroyed that, how he had even poisoned her friends in the house against her.

When both parties felt fully appraised of the other's stories, Valeria finally felt ready to return to the drawing room and to meet Allen again. Perhaps even to forgive a little.

CHAPTER TWELVE

Until Valeria reappeared, Allen had been truly happy in his new home. The work was hard but the pay was fair and he was safe. He was off the streets and treated with real kindness by Mr Richmond and Nora, who despite her new role as his employer insisted that he stand on no ceremony.

He was proud of the work he was doing. It was the kind of thing he could do well. Taking as it did both strength for the heavier lifting and a delicacy and coordinated touch for the many highly sensitive instruments he had noted on his first arrival.

But that sense of value in himself had evaporated when Valeria came screaming at him. He had, for so long, convinced himself that he had done all he could to protect her. That his invasion of Miss Umbridge's home was nothing more than an attempt to protect her from the violent retaliation of Taylor. He no longer felt that way, now he was filled with guilt and worried that he had destroyed her feelings for him. Whatever they may have been, the loss of them weighed heavily on him.

Valeria had apologised for her outburst and he had begged forgiveness for his many sins. Even so, the sting of the hatred in the look she had given him weighed on his mind in the days that followed.

He was pondering this while carefully cleaning the inner workings of one of Mr Richmond's most precise chronometers. Despite the delicate work he was hurrying to get the parts back together in time to set the time by the drop of the ball from Greenwich's flagpole. This occurred at one o'clock post meridiem each day and was accompanied by a cannon shot that was easily heard even here off Baker Street.

He was carefully placing the spring mechanism back against the baseplate and screwing in the frictionless coupling when Valeria entered the room. Pretending to be concentrating on his task, he kept his head down.

If only it could be as easy to put their friendship back together as it was with this timekeeper.

Valeria collected some papers and began filing them. Allen knew she must be running some errand for Mr Richmond.

"Nora insists you stop acting like a maid around here, you are her guest, you know," he said gently.

"I can work for my room and board as easily as you can."

She didn't sound angry, but there was a tension in her voice, a forced politeness. It felt like a brick wall between them after the intimacy of their talk that day she had walked him back to Miss Umbridge's.

"I know the feeling," he said.

"What feeling?"

"That one cannot shake where one came from. That Miss June used you as a slave and so you feel like one. I sometimes see it in how Nora speaks to her husband, but why should we feel so inferior?"

"You should feel so inferior because you are a thief. I feel it because it is how a woman, especially the poor are raised up to feel. Even Nora is seen as her husband's property. She proposes scientific ideas and designs experiments, but nowhere in the publications of the Royal Society or the Athenaeum will you ever see the name Nora Richmond."

Allen scratched his head. He had been trying to talk about Valeria and Allen, but somehow this had become about the whole body of man and woman-kind.

"I suppose so," he answered, not entirely sure what he was agreeing to.

Valeria went back to stacking papers. She looked every bit as beautiful as he remembered and a pang of something else pricked the ball of shame that seemed to have settled in his stomach.

He felt a powerful urge to keep the conversation going. To hear her voice, to make her laugh. Eventually, he settled on the most straightforward question of all.

"What do you mean? Nora is his property. They seem so—"

"That has been woman's lot. We are considered the property of our husbands... if we have them. We are undereducated and then treated as if we are stupid. Beaten by the physical strength of men, then told we are fundamentally weak. Miss Umbridge had a large library of revolutionary texts. They did much to expand my understanding."

"I would want a woman who was equal to me," Allen offered, hoping this was the right answer.

"It is easy enough to say, even Mr Richmond claims to want that, but he is also blind to the ways in which he has failed to allow Nora equality. It is very like how I cannot accept their charity, so I do whatever housework is available to keep me busy. I will no doubt have to find myself a husband if I wish to get out from under Nora's kindness. There is no other option for a woman. We do not get to live in bachelorhood as men do."

Allen considered this for a moment. It seemed odd to think of Valeria living alone in a house of her own. Though he wasn't sure if that was because she was a woman or because he couldn't stop imagining the man she would live with being himself. Once more he was filled with guilt. Having ruined her life it was unlikely that she would ever accept him. Even if she did, what did he have to offer?!

"Perhaps Nora can find you someone of Mr Richmond's ilk to keep you, at the very least, in a comfortable cage."

Valeria laughed, a genuine cheerful laugh that filled Allen up with joy. "Yes, someone rich and very, very old that I might avoid his grasp through quickness of feet and enjoy a long widowhood when time has run its course with him."

Allen laughed too and felt the wall between them come down. They spoke naturally now, as they had of old. Soon their respective works were forgotten until, with the clock still not reassembled the bang of the Greenwich gun brought them back to earth.

The difference in their attitudes to each other was no flash in the pan. They talked for hours while Allen got back to work and Valeria got back to being a guest rather than a maid. The afternoon flew by as they chatted.

Over dinner they enjoyed an exchange of jokes and anecdotes at the dinner table where they now ate with Mr and Mrs Richmond. Occasionally, the couple exchanged amused glances that he felt were almost certainly at his and Valeria's expense.

Since she had no real chores of her own Valeria shifted to helping Allen with his. There were some delightful days in the laboratories when all four of them were working in concert. Sometimes with Stephen, distraught at the mess on entering the room. The grumpy man would attempt to clean up, giving up and leaving only to repeat the attempt after an hour or so. Allen assumed he spent that hour recovering in the regions of the house where his sway kept all in order.

As the days passed Allen found himself spending all the time he could with Valeria. Taking tea with her, assisting her with carrying the shopping when she went to the market, and dragging out mealtimes when they would be sat together talking.

Even when they were together there was still some desire driving him to lean in more, to pay more attention. He longed to hold her hand, thrilled when he was able to assist her with something that allowed him to place a hand on her waist, or when she linked her arm with his on a walk.

He would gladly have died or — more likely — killed to kiss her.

In the evenings she would sit in the drawing room and read by gaslight, and he would sit and struggle to follow the words on the page. At first, he was embarrassed that he could hardly read, but when it became clear that Valeria was pleased to teach him, he played it up, taking pleasure in her joy in his every small advancement in literacy.

Strangely, the moments he felt he understood his own feelings most were when he would work with Mr Richmond. William would talk about some new discovery. There was that intoxicated joy in his passion for the unknown that seemed to match the intensity of Allen's feelings for Valeria.

Day after day passed and he felt his feelings growing and growing and yet he feared to make them actions. Instead, he did all he could to make her happy, and left it at that. Simply hovering about her. As time went on, something in his inability to act felt deeply unmanly to him.

Mr Richmond had used the word inertia to describe the way in which an object that was still would remain so until pushed. Somehow, that was Allen's feeling, that he was unable to move, to act without an outside push. Some signal or force from Valeria.

And so, he was as happy as he'd ever been and as miserable as he had ever been all in one.

CHAPTER THIRTEEN

Valeria watched Nora struggling to decide between two bonnets for the third time that day and offered the same advice she had offered the previous two times. "Take both with you, Nora."

"If I take your advice, I will end up moving my full wardrobe from London up to Hamley-on-Thames. I am already an object of ridicule to these people, I would dread to give them further ammunition."

"Why do you worry what William's family think? You have not married them. In fact, merely attending is all you can possibly be required to do by your husband. It is not on you to change their minds, but on them to beg your forgiveness for how they have treated you."

"Oh, Valeria. But I must do my best. William loves his family and we may well need allies within the inner circle. There are cousins and siblings galore who are working to have him disinherited, and to take whatever they can from him. I could not bear to see him reduced in circumstances for no other sin than his loving me and I loving him."

"You are too good a person, Nora. Do not expect much from these people, they are calcified old hags and bores. They will look down on the poor until the very day the revolution tears their castles from them and feeds them to the hounds."

"You do talk so foolishly, Valeria. What do you suppose your revolutionaries would do with me? Wife of a Richmond? It is my head beneath the guillotine too."

Valeria laughed. "I doubt very much that we shall see such a revolution here. But do not give too much value to the opinions of these people so long as your husband's opinion of you remains as adoring as it is now."

She took Nora's hand in hers.

"Oh, Valeria. Will you be all right with me gone? I could arrange to stay. Someone must host our guests."

"No, you go press the flesh and win your husband some allies with your charms. Allen and Stephen will look after me."

"Aye. I suspect that Allen would do more than that for you if you were to give him an indication."

Valeria felt herself blushing. "Don't be foolish, we are but friends." She almost believed it too, but was unable to keep the hope out of her voice when she asked, "What do you mean, an indication?"

"Oh, surely you can't be blind to his affections."

Valeria scoured her mind, looking for some indication, something in his manner that might match up with Nora's suggestion. Certainly, he enjoyed spending time with her, but he had given no sign beyond that. Never spoken a sweet nothing, though she had — and she found it hard to admit even to herself — often imagined sweet nothings spoken to her in his voice.

"What signs are you seeing in him that I seem to be so blind to?" Valeria asked.

Nora tutted in that oddly motherly way she had now that she was married. The one that made Valeria feel almost like her child despite the fact that she was two years older than her friend.

"I have never seen a boy so obviously in love with a woman, let us leave it at that. You should either put him out of his misery, or," and at this Nora's face broke into a mischievous grin, "you should give him some deliberate sign of encouragement."

* * *

Nora and William left the next day leaving Valeria in charge of the house and Allen with a long list of chores to keep the labs running while they were away. Stephen seemed absolutely ecstatic to see them go. Perhaps he would have a chance to finally bring the labs back into a state of near civilisation and perhaps even total cleanliness.

Valeria waved the couple off from the doorway and once their coach had rounded the corner and disappeared up Baker Street she returned to the house.

In the silence of the hallway she pondered for a moment what Nora had said about Allen.

A deliberate sign, she thought to herself. Repeating the words aloud to the gaslight on the wall beside her head.

Then she went upstairs.

Allen was playing with the newly born monkey, which had reached the age where it was finally jumping about away from the protection of its parents. He would often take it out of the cage and let it cling to the weft of his coat the way it would cling to its mother's breast.

He was talking to it as if it were a human, and pretending that its squeaks were some sort of conversational reply.

"Well, of course, little sir," Allen said. "You may very well say such a thing not having any investment in the Empire, but this mutiny in India might well affect my ability to feed you such treats as dried dates... Yes, I thought that might grab your attention..."

"Might I interrupt?" Valeria asked.

Allen turned and gave her a broad smile. "Of course, I was just catching this little chap up on all the current affairs that I *read* in the Times this morning."

Valeria laughed a little. He was very proud of the progress he was making with his reading and had taken to reading the newspaper in the morning. She idly seized a small grape from the bunch on the desk and offered it to the monkey.

The monkey refused. No doubt already spoiled by Allen who had taken on nearly as protective a role for the little creature as its own parents. They watched Allen disapprovingly from their cage.

She grabbed a few more grapes and fed them to the grown-up monkeys while Allen chatted idly about the situation in India and the latest Parliamentary scandal.

A deliberate sign, she thought. Wondering what it should be. For a moment she pictured herself saying, very matter of factly, "Allen, do be quiet and kiss me."

The imagined look of shock on his face made her chuckle to herself as she watched one of the monkeys bite a grape in half and pass the other half to his beloved. Yes, she would just turn around and bold as brass tell him then and there to stop fooling around and kiss her.

Instead she stood there fooling around herself.

Just a moment, she thought. A moment to build my courage.

She pushed another grape between the bars, took a deep breath and turned.

"Allen," she said.

"Yes?"

"Do stop fooling around and—" The door opened, cutting her off, as Stephen ploughed into the room a look of grim determination on his face.

As if to underline the sudden shift in mood in the room, the little monkey began without the slightest hint of shame to urinate liberally down Allen's jacket.

When she had finished laughing and Allen had put the monkey back in the cage, she stood behind him and pulled his jacket off. The sink in the animal lab was full so they went next door so she could soak it in the chemical lab. Stephen remained behind and with great glee began to dust everything in the room.

The chemical lab's many pungent smells went a long way to covering up the smell on the jacket. Valeria ran some cold water over the damp patch and held the jacket under the tap for several minutes.

Allen was laughing charmingly about the situation. "That silly critter. What was it you were about to say?" he asked.

Valeria felt her cheeks blush. "What do you mean?"

She focused very hard on scrubbing the coat, although she knew it could make little difference.

"You were about to say something. Your face went very serious and you said 'Do stop fooling around and...' and then Stephen arrived. You looked like you were about to tell me I was dying."

"It was just about..." she was about to lie, but suddenly realised that her scrubbing away at this coat seemed oddly similar to the way Allen would sometimes get so focused on a task when she entered a room or she caught him looking in her direction.

Light began to dawn in her head. She let the coat fall into the sink and turned to him.

"I was going to tell you to stop fooling around," her heart leapt into her throat. "And... and I forget what else."

Then the sink began to overflow and Allen pushed her gently aside, grabbing his coat from the sink. Without the cloth blocking the plug the water began to subside.

Stephen poked his head around the door and looked at the water on the floor.

"You best clear that spill up, Allen." He looked between them with his usual angry look on his face and seemed about to ask a question, then thought better of it and vanished.

CHAPTER FOURTEEN

From then they had talked all day, just as they normally did but nothing had really been said. Eventually she retired to bed, but sleep just would not come.

She felt so foolish, cursing herself for missing the moment, the moment to make the decisive sign that would change her relationship and her life.

Then Valeria heard the sharp crack of a hammer and the tinkle of glass on the floor from the front of the house. She sat bolt upright, a sick feeling coming over her. For a moment she was back in Miss Umbridge's house waiting to hear the over-sprung bolt of the library bang once more.

How could this be happening again? Her only calming thought was that it could not be Allen this time. She got out of bed and opened her bedroom door and crept to the landing. Looking down she could see the front door ajar a pane of glass smashed through to allow someone to turn the latch. Wherever they were they had moved on, deeper into the house.

She began to creep downstairs. If she could reach the servants quarters without alerting the intruders, she could wake Allen and Stephen to scare the thieves off.

She paused at the open door of the dining room. Peering around the corner she could see a man carefully placing something on the mantelpiece. He appeared to have already filled a bag with the candlesticks and silver from about the room.

She slipped past the dining room door and into the servants' quarters. She opened Stephen's door first and slipped in. His face seemed almost to be smiling in his sleep. The moment she shook him awake that changed and his familiar look of deep seeded irritation set in. She whispered the situation to him and he told her to wait here.

He went quietly next door and woke Allen.

Valeria couldn't bear to sit there waiting to hear what happened next so she followed the men at a safe distance. They moved like shadows through the dark, Stephen a little louder than Allen. Then they vanished through the dining room door. A moment later there was an almighty shout and the sound of china breaking.

She rushed to the door and looked in. Allen was wrestling the man face on while Stephen had his hand around the man's neck from behind. For a moment it looked like all would be well. That a short quick tussle would bring the man to his knees.

Then she saw the flash of moonlight on the man's blade and screamed.

There was the sound of cloth tearing and the man broke free from Allen who threw himself backwards to the floor. The fall took Stephen with him and the man wriggled free. He was the first up and made for the pantry.

The back door slammed shut and he was gone.

All Valeria could hear in the dark was the harsh

breathing of Allen, Stephen and herself and the drip-drip-drip sound of some spillage.

She looked about for a match and lit the lamp turning it up as bright as possible. Stephen and Allen stood on either side of the mantelpiece leaning on it, catching their breath.

The dripping continued.

Stephen was examining something on the mantelpiece. He picked it up, a flash of yellow paper.

"Thank you, Allen," he read aloud. "See Taylor for your share."

Stephen walked over to the lamp, lifted the glass and lit the paper on fire.

"I suppose they planned to frame you then," he said, turning to look at Allen.

Valeria saw the look on Stephen's face turn from anger to fear and followed his gaze.

Allen's face was pale and he looked ready to collapse. His shirt was bright red across his chest and Valeria could now see that the dripping sound came from the blood which was dripping from the saturated cloth.

Valeria screamed and felt herself going faint.

No, she thought. He needs me.

"I... I'll get a doctor," she said hurrying to grab her coat and boots.

CHAPTER FIFTEEN

Allen was being chased through the streets of London by dogs, huge hell hounds with nasty knife-like teeth and glowing coals for eyes. They had escaped from one of the circles of hell and had been given his scent by Taylor.

He was not sure how he knew this, but he knew it with all certainty.

Somehow, he just knew that Taylor had sent them, though he was unsure of the how's or whys of how Taylor kept control of the beasts. Perhaps if he could work that out, he could take control of the hounds himself, and turn them back on his hunter. Until then, his only chance was to stay ahead of the hounds long enough to figure this all out.

He didn't recognise any of the streets he was running down so he used his usual strategy when he got lost. He headed uphill. When he found a vantage point, he'd look for a spire. He knew all the churches in London so any spire would be a dead giveaway of his location. From there it would be easy to head for somewhere safe. Somewhere near Baker Street.

He took a corner that looked like it would take him up a steep incline, and was surprised to see Valeria ahead of him. She was standing alone in a street, calling out his name. Only it was not her voice but something close to the half-remembered voice of his mother. He tried to yell for her to turn around but his throat was constricted, bound up by whatever horror silences voices in a dream.

So, he ran towards her, willing her to get off the street to safety, but she would not turn and continued to call his name loudly, drawing in the baying hounds. He needed her to be safe. He needed her to hide, or else the hounds would catch them both.

Eventually, he was almost close enough to touch her. That was when he felt the teeth sink into his side. He looked down and saw that the huge jaws of one of the hounds was holding his flesh. One large incisor was driven firmly into his side just below his left rib.

He screamed silently once more, and woke up.

Though the world of the dream faded, the pain did not. There was still a violent pain just below his left rib, an agonising pain that would not leave him the way the phantom dogs and the incarnation of Valeria that spoke in his mother's voice had done so.

He looked around him trying to ground himself in this reality and send the pain back into the world of the dream.

His room surrounded him, the familiar one under Nora's roof. The servants quarters. He knew that there was a maid sleeping one room over on one side and Stephen sleeping one room over on the other. This helped to ground him a little, and the fear of the dream began to subside.

For some reason, he had for a moment been sure he would awake in Taylor's new rooms wherever they were. That he would wake in whatever new hideout Taylor had sent men from to ravage Allen's new home.

But he was safe, home even.

He turned his head the other way and saw that Valeria was there, sat beside his bedside. Sleeping calmly, not set upon by hell hounds or calling out in someone else's voice.

She must have been there a while, from how dishevelled she looked. She was slumped forward and had fallen asleep with her hair in complete disarray. He had a tender urge to reach out and brush the tangles from it.

She had her nightgown on but her legs were still jammed into a pair of walking boots.

He smiled to see her there, beautiful even in that state of disarray and undress. He tried to sit up and stopped immediately. The pain of the dreamed dog bite exploded in his side.

Lying there for a moment, he tried not to sob in case he woke Valeria.

When the pain had subsided a little, with far greater care, he lifted his blanket to see the damage. A wide bandage was bound tightly across his midriff. On his left side a thick pad of absorbent cotton marked the site of his injury.

That explained the boots, Valeria must have been the one to run for the doctor... and the doctor would explain the strange dreams and how hard they were to shake. So, he had been injured and given a tincture of opium, or possibly something a little stronger even than that.

That would explain too why his memory was so fuzzy, he thought.

It took him a moment to remember that it had been the shadowy intruder who had done this injury to him, not the dreamed-up pack of dogs. Though it was true enough that Taylor had sent the man. He had no doubt of that, even in dreams then some nugget of truth could be fished out if you panned hard enough.

In his mind he replayed the moment it had happened. The shriek from Valeria, and the sickening feeling that something had happened to her. That there had been a second man and that Taylor was making good his threat of months ago to send someone to "break" Valeria if he failed to rob the Umbridge place.

He could remember the moment of relief when he saw she was okay and the moment of panic, less than a second later — the feel of the man's wrist breaking free and knowing that he was brandishing a knife in anger. Then the blow that had felt at first like a punch, the sort he might easily walk away from with nothing more than some bruising. Then the cold, a few moments later that horrible spreading, stinging cold which exploded in his side and brought with it a feeling of nausea and of pain.

Then it all became fuzzy again. Fragmentary. The feeling of pain and of floating. Hearing reassuring words, first in Stephen's voice — "Miss Collins has gone for the doctor... hold on... stay awake, boy..." — then in the voice of the doctor what seemed like weeks or months later, but must have been only earlier this night.

Then a deep black from which he could pull no meaning or memory.

And then he was running with the dogs in hot pursuit.

Could it only be a few hours later? The fres[h]
the pain in his side seemed to suggest so. [It]
felt so long ago, faded memories bleached by the sun and by time.

The effort of remembering was exhausting and thought was slow and difficult. So, since there was little else to do for now, he gave up on thinking out the problem. And decided he would wait to be told of all that might have happened while he was knocked out cold.

Valeria was safe, he was in his bed, all would be well, injury or no. Even if that was just the opium talking, he was not concerned.

He lay there and smiled at Valeria as she slept, letting his mind simply run and run over nothing but her face. He'd be asleep soon he imagined, so why not enjoy her presence as long as he could stay awake.

She shifted a little and yawned, like a dog chasing rabbits in its sleep.

He wondered what she was dreaming of, if he was in the worlds her mind was creating in the same way she was in his dreams.

She let out a little sneeze and set up straight suddenly. Her eyes remained closed but she stretched in the way of someone reluctantly awake.

He closed his eyes and lay back, pretending to be asleep.

He heard her stretch again and then sit forward. Her breathing changed from sleep to wake, and then to watchful. The chair creaked as she got up, and then the floorboards did the same as she came closer. He could tell she was close enough that he could reach out and touch her, it would look like an accident. He just wanted to feel her there, for him. And then her hand closed on his. His heart began thudding in his chest and breathing became difficult, like he'd forgotten the simple process of pumping his ribs to draw in air.

Every nerve in his body was switched off except for those in the palm of his hand where she touched him, held him.

She whispered close to him, "Be well, my love."

Had he heard that right? Her love?

He snapped his eyes open and she gasped a little.

She was leaning forward, her face so close to his that he could almost taste her breath.

"Hello, my love," he said. Immediately he regretted it. She most likely meant it merely as a phrase, or in a platonic way, perhaps the way the publican's wives would always call him "love" when he was young enough. Before they had started treating him mean when he had grown old enough to be considered a nuisance.

She stood stock still for what seemed far too long. Staring down at him. *What was she thinking?* he wondered. *What should he say?*

"Very well," she said.

It was in a tone that he was not quite sure how to interpret. And in fact, the words seemed not to be aimed at him, but at herself.

"How is this for a deliberate sign of encouragement?"

"What do you—" he did not finish the question because she leaned in as he spoke and stoppered up his mouth with hers. Their two faces met in a long, passionate kiss where he drifted to heaven and was held there by her sweet kiss. For how long he couldn't tell, but he never wanted it to end. The kiss could have been for a moment or longer than the strange black gulf he had lost his memories into.

She leaned forward so he didn't need to prop himself up at all, pushing him back into the pillow. Their breath became ragged, their kissing more passionate. She pulled away and he could feel her breath coming out of her, more and more frantic driven by surprise at what she'd done and the passion with which they were both drawn into.

Then he looked her in the eyes and smiled. His hand cupped her cheek, his other went to her waist and he pulled her close, pressing his mouth against hers once again. They stayed like that for what felt like an age, the whole world vanishing as they held each other in their arms.

When they finally broke apart, she looked down at him and said, "I would have died if you hadn't made it."

He smiled back at her. "I had no idea you felt this way."

His mind was racing, how long had she felt this way, or was this some act of kindness to a dying man. He decided very quickly that he did not care one jot if it was. Better to die happy.

"What happened exactly?" he asked.

She sat on the side of his bed and held his hand.

"It turns out Mr Taylor found out you were living here. Inspector Lamond called around earlier and told us this."

Then she launched into an account of what had happened. It turned out that Mr Richmond had been hunting Taylor all over London with the help of one Inspector Lamond. After a particularly rough run in, Taylor's man had followed Mr Richmond home.

Taylor put a man on watch outside the house and soon found out that Allen was living there. Taylor then had the man break in and try, in a rather crude way, to frame Allen, as a way of avenging himself on Allen for leaving the gang.

Allen's heart sank. "After last night, we're not safe," he said. "He'll send another man. Perhaps to do some real violence."

"No, he won't," Valeria said squeezing his hands gently.

"Why not? What do you know that I don't?"

"Oh, all sorts of things. Most importantly though that Inspector Lamond had a man watching the house too. He followed the intruder through the streets all the way back to Mr Taylor's. Then rushed back here where Inspector Lamond was being of immense use to the doctor in helping to keep you alive. His jacket was as drenched in blood when they were done as some cutthroat, he might have tossed in gaol himself"

"But Taylor?"

"I am getting to that. Lamond's man comes back with the address and off rushes Lamond to load up a cart with every bobby in the district. They'll be arresting Taylor as we speak, I imagine, if it's not already done."

Could it all be over? he thought to himself. *Was he finally safe from Taylor's machinations?* He had so many questions, and they all seemed to spill out of him faster than Valeria could attempt to answer them.

With a look of almost comical irritation on her face she leaned in and kissed him again, shutting him up.

He suddenly realised with a shock of scandal that here they were, unchaperoned in his bedroom, both in a state of some undress. He without a shirt, she in just her nightgown. He was aware of their bodies in a way he had not been until then.

"You should go," he said. "What would Stephen think if he were to walk in on this?"

"Goodness," she laughed. "I don't think he'd suspect you of being much threat to my honour in the state you're in."

"Oh, but I could be," he said, smiling what he hoped was a wicked smile.

She kissed him again, and when she was done, she said, "Calm yourself. Get some sleep. I'll be back in the morning and we can discuss this more over breakfast. For now, though, the doctor said rest was absolutely vital."

Allen couldn't sleep when she left him to sleep in her own bed that night. He was too excited. His mind kept rushing over and over the events of the evening. Somehow, being stabbed seemed far less an ordeal than simply being awake and being loved.

He lay in bed and remembered each one, the flood of emotions that felt so intense they seemed to colour the world around them.

One feeling predominated over all the others — utter joy.

He loved her and she loved him; no matter what life threw at him from now onward, they would be happy.

*** * *

IF YOU MISSED any books in this series:

The Orphan's Courage

The Orphan's Hope

The Mother's Secret

The Maid's Blessing

THE BEGGAR'S DREAM PREVIEW

It was a cold, rainy night in London. Abigail picked up the blackened old poker which leaned like a crooked old man against the small fireplace. Giving the burning embers a prod, she managed to get a bit more life going in the fire. Shuffling a little closer she wondered how long it would last as she tried to soak up the warmth as best she could.

If she closed her eyes, she could almost imagine she was relaxing inside her very own townhouse after a long but rewarding day at her shop. Her blonde hair would be pinned above her head in ringlets that curled around her face. The day had been spent sewing dresses for the most important ladies of London. Perhaps Miles would be by her side, and they would hold hands in front of the fire, lazily enjoying their time together after a lavish meal.

The sound of her father's hacking cough brought her back to reality. Garth Patrick was sat on their only chair with his one leg propped up on an old crate that Abigail had found on the street. He was using it in place of a footstool.

"Are you okay, Father?" Abigail got to her feet and reached up to feel the temperature of his forehead. She brushed away the damp blond locks from his forehead and could see that his brown eyes were bloodshot. He had once told her that her blue eyes matched her mother's. How she wished that she was here now to turn to.

"Oh, I'm fine, my dear, nothing to worry about it," he croaked.

Despite his insistence, it was something to worry about indeed. His forehead was burning and he was sweating through his clothes, yet shivering at the same time. Abigail was in no doubt that it was a fever. She gave him a reproachful look before she moved back to the fire to tend to the pot of broth.

It contained the last of their food, every little scrap

from the tiny kitchen at the back of their one-roomed home. Round and round she stirred, but the broth was getting no thicker. With a slight sigh she carefully poured it out into a bowl. Making sure not to spill a drop, she placed it on the table which was made from another crate with a rag placed over it, to try and make it look a little nicer. Her father tried to lean forward so that he could taste some but Abigail could see it took all of his strength to make the slight movement.

"No, Father, just you sit and relax, I'll help you," she said, gently pushing him back so that he was resting against the back of the chair. Slowly, she began to spoon the meager, watery broth into his mouth. With each spoonful she silently prayed that it would at least settle his hunger and allow him to get some of his strength back.

"I'm sorry, Abigail," he said sadly, "for not being able to give you the life you deserve."

Abigail opened her mouth to protest.

He waved a hand at her, cutting off the words that sat heavy in her throat. Then his sad eyes glanced around at their dismal surroundings. They had struggled for as long as Abigail could remember. They had been lucky to get these lodgings in East London. The small room being on the ground floor provided a huge relief to her father who had only the one leg. Their place was small and cramped and the rent was low, but it was still a struggle to get by.

"You know, things were different when your mother was still alive." He leaned his head back in the chair, having finished supping the last of the broth and launched into a story with a faraway look in his eyes and a glimmer of a smile.

"We were young and very much in love. I'll never forget the first time we met. I was dressed in my red uniform, all new and freshly pressed, proudly riding my horse on my way to battle. Your mother was feeding an apple to her own horse over the fence and stroking its nose as I rode by. I called out "are you lost, m'lady?" with a cheeky grin. "She whirled around, her hands on her hips and put me in my place: *'I should think not. You're the stranger around here.'*"

A sigh escaped him and she thought she saw the shine of tears in his eyes.

"In an instant I was smitten, she was a right beauty and with a bit of spark in her too. I apologised, playing humble, and got down from my horse to introduce myself properly. Oh, I can't tell you how she made me feel. Maybe it was going to war but I think she was just special... your mother. I rode away promising to write to her and sure as anything I kept my word. Her letters kept me going during the tough times of war. Giving me hope and something to fight for. I arrived home victorious and we were soon married."

A cough stopped the story for a few moments but Abigail was spellbound and wanted to hear more. "Tell me all about it," she said when the cough subsided.

"Well, sadly, Wendy's family weren't happy about the match, I can tell you. The Dunkley family were gentry you see and your mother was supposed to be married off to a Lord, not a poor soldier. We were too in love to care about what they thought so we eloped and they all but cut her off for it.

"After a while, her parents' disapproval weighed heavy on Wendy and she spoke to them. Eventually, Mrs Dunkley could see that Wendy was happy and that I would do anything for her daughter. They didn't welcome me into the family with open arms but agreed to provide some of Wendy's inheritance so that she could have some semblance of a life fitting for a lady.

"We got set up in a beautiful cottage in the countryside. Pretty flowers decorated the garden, we had fields and a stable for horses and your mother made the whole place a home. And just in time too, for you came along shortly after.

"The spitting image of your mother you were, we were a happy family for those first five years, until duty called and I was sent away to war once more. Wendy hated it when I had to leave but I was filled with pride and determination to defend my country for my two girls at home. Even so, I ached to be away from you both. It felt like all my wildest dreams had come true." He paused for a moment, deep in thought before his indulgent smile faded slightly, turning into longing and sadness.

"But during one battle I was... struck down, losing my leg and was sent home for good, no longer able to fulfil my duties as a soldier. With some difficulty we got by, Wendy having occasional help from her parents and I eventually managed to secure a bit of work keeping accounts at the local shop.

"Everything looked like it was going to be okay until that terrible day when your mother died in a horse-riding accident. The Dunkleys cut us off completely, raising the rent on the cottage so that we were forced to move. Crippled and carrying what little belongings I could, I took us into the city and found us room and board in a crumbling old Inn. It took me weeks to secure the job with Mr Walter and by that point all our savings were nearly gone."

Abigail didn't need to hear the rest, she knew how the story went, her hollow stomach rumbled loudly as if to remind her. It had been nice to know more about her mother, though. She'd never heard her father speak about the life they used to have before. His words interrupted her thoughts and she turned back to him. Then she could see that it was the light of love that lit his eyes and she prayed that one day she too would feel that light.

"You look more and more like your mother every day," her father said fondly.

Abigail smiled, filled with pride. There was a picture

of her mother with her father and Abigail as a baby above the fireplace. Her mother had been very beautiful and her father was lit up with more joy than she'd ever seen on his face. They looked like something out of a fairy tale, so far removed from the life Abigail knew now.

A loud cough interrupted Abigail from her thoughts.

"I think it's time for my medicine," her father wheezed. He was often in poor health, blaming the damp walls, the smoky air and the diseased rats which populated the city.

Abigail jumped up from her spot on the floor in front of the fire and fetched the bottle of medicine from the shelf. With great care, she measured out the foul-smelling liquid into a cup and held it out to her father.

"Thanks, Abigail," he said, pushing himself up with a groan and taking the cup from her with a shaking hand. He gulped it back in one go, his face screwed up in disgust, "It's lovely stuff."

She laughed, relieved that he still had a sense of humour.

"I think that's bedtime, Abi," he said pointedly.

She wasn't sleepy but there was little point trying to stay up with an empty stomach.

She picked up his walking sticks and held them out so that he could get up out of the chair. As he pulled himself up to hop across the small room Abigail was relieved to see that there was a bit of colour in his previously white cheeks. Though, he was a long way off looking healthy, with his bony frame, and the permanent shadows under his eyes.

"I can take the floor this time," he offered but his insistence was half-hearted and she shook her head.

"No, Father, you need your rest or all that medicine will go to waste." She knew how hard he worked, but he got little in return and he was always complaining about how expensive the medicine was.

After he got into their only bed, he said goodnight and closed his eyes. Abigail moved quietly back to the front of the fireplace. The fire was simmering down but it was still nice and warm so she got as cosy as she could with the ragged grey blanket. She was used to the floor though at times she dreamed of feather beds and cotton sheets. These were things she would have one day, but more importantly she would have food.

As she closed her eyes, she daydreamed wistfully about the life her father had narrated, imagining how different things might be if her mother was still alive. It was so far removed from their real lives. One where they had no food to wake up to, her father was sick with a fever and she was all he had.

Tomorrow would be better, she told herself, she would get work in the shop, have enough pennies to bring something home for dinner and they'd make it to the end of the day without rumbling bellies and the enduring ache of despair that came with constant hunger.

Just a few more years working in the dress shop and she'd be qualified to be a top seamstress. Then, when she was old enough, she'd be able to inherit the shop and be in charge of designing the really expensive pretty dresses that the rich ladies wore. She was always in awe of the fitted, flowing gowns she saw them wearing, imagining that one day she could look like a princess too and then she'd sweep Miles off his feet just like her mum did with her father.

Closing her eyes and rolling over, she wriggled around until she was comfortable enough, listening to the soft snoring of her father and the rumbling of her empty stomach. She wished that her daydreams would all come true, that she could have a nice warm bed to sleep in and enough food so that they never went hungry.

Eventually, the shouts from the streets outside and the stomping of footsteps upstairs faded out as Abigail drifted off into sleep. Her dreams were filled with her mother's smiling face. Then her mother was walking away. Each time she turned a corner she was wearing a different dress. They were all so beautiful, embroidered with ribbon. Abigail kept running through the dirt-laden streets but she could never catch up. Panting and with tears running down her face she caught a glance of her own reflection in the window of the grocer. Her face dirty with soot and her stained white dress looking like a ragged old sack.

Her shabby reflection was replaced with the sight of a loaf of bread, displayed proudly in the window. It looked so tasty and she could smell the freshly baked scent wafting out through the open door. It made her mouth water and her stomach growl with desperation. Her hand reached out to grab it but the Baker yelled out and shook his broomstick at her.

"Get out of here, you dirty vagrant."

The words echoed in her mind and she had to sniff back her tears. Soon all was quiet, her father's snores easing into deep breathing as he rolled over onto his side. Abigail curled up in a ball and basked in the subtle glow as the fire finally faded out, leading the way to a soothing dreamless sleep.

Find out what happens to Abigail in The Beggar's Dream FREE with Kindle Unlimited or just 0.99p

THANKS FOR READING

I love sharing my Victorian Romances with you and have several more waiting for my editor to approve. Join my Newsletter by clicking here to find out when my books are available.

I want to thank you so much for reading this book, if you enjoyed it please leave a review on Amazon. It makes such a difference to me and I would be so grateful.

Thank you so much.

Sadie

Previous Books:

THANKS FOR READING

The Beggar's Dream

The Orphan's Courage

The Orphan's Hope

The Mother's Secret

The Maid's Blessing

ABOUT THE AUTHOR

Sadie Hope was born in Preston, Lancashire, where she worked in a textile factory for many years. Married with two grown children, she would spend her nights writing stories about life in Victorian times. She loved to read all the books of this era and often found herself daydreaming of characters that would pop into her head.

She hopes you enjoy these stories for she has many more to share with you.

Follow Sadie on Facebook

Follow Sadie on Amazon

©Copyright 2019 Sadie Hope
All Rights Reserved

License Notes

This eBook is licensed for personal enjoyment only. It may not be resold. Your continued respect for author's rights is appreciated.

This story is a work of fiction any resemblance to people is purely coincidence. All places, names, events, businesses, etc. are used in a fictional manner. All characters are from the imagination of the author.

The end

Printed in Great Britain
by Amazon